Ace and Christi Series

Grandpa's Christmas Gift

by

Sarah Hopewell

Illustrated by

John Truman

Lewisville, Texas

Poem "The Christ of Christmas" by
Eugene M. Harrison from *742 Heart-Warming Poems*
compiled by John R. Rice, Sword of the Lord
Publications, Murfreesboro, TN

Accelerated Christian Education
P.O. Box 299000
Lewisville, Texas 75029-9000

Reprinted 2012

ISBN 1-56265-073-4
4 5 6 7 8 Printing/Year 16 15 14 13 12
Printed in the United States of America

TABLE OF CONTENTS

Chapter	Page
1. Night Call	5
2. Screeching Sirens	13
3. Cold Ride	19
4. In Good Hands	23
5. New Friends	31
6. News	43
7. Detective on the Loose	55
8. God of the Impossible	59
9. A Good Report	69
10. A Challenging Opportunity	75
11. Work to Do	83
12. Helping Hands	95
13. Wags	109
14. Homecoming	115
15. Time Together	123
16. The Surprise	131
17. Another Snow	139
18. God in Control	145
19. A Visit to the Farm	157
20. Fun and Preparation	167
21. Safe Deliveries	171
22. A Reason to Celebrate	181

CHAPTER 1

NIGHT CALL

Like a ship struggling through fog, Ace Virtueson fought to open his eyes and untangle his puzzled brain. *It must be the middle of the night,* he thought. He turned and looked at the clock on his nightstand and saw that the red numbers read 1:53. It **was** the middle of the night! *What woke me up?* Then there were scuffling feet in the hall, and whispers. *A burglar?* No, it was his father's voice. That was strange. *What is my dad doing up?* But before he could come up with an answer, the bedroom door suddenly swung open, and Mr. and Mrs. Virtueson, silhouetted by the hall light, quickly crossed the room to his bedside. Mrs. Virtueson switched on the small reading lamp on the nightstand, and Ace held his breath.

"Ace," his father urgently whispered. "I am sorry to waken you, but you must get up." His tone was pressing—not quite panicky, but determined and explicit. There seemed to be cause for alarm, and Ace sat straight up in his bed, still puzzled. It was then he noticed that both parents were already dressed rather than being in their nightclothes as should be expected at 1:53 in the morning.

"What is wrong? Why are we getting up in the middle of the night?" he asked. "Why are you two dressed?"

Mrs. Virtueson sat down gently on the edge of her son's bed and put her hand on his arm. There was urgency in her voice as well. "Ace, Grandpa became very ill tonight, and right now an ambulance is taking him to the hospital." She paused and dabbed at the corner of one eye. "Grandma phoned about ten minutes ago, and they are on their way to Highland Hospital right now."

Ace gasped. So that was it. There had been a crisis at the farm. All kinds of questions immediately popped to the front of his mind; but before he could ask any of them, Mr. Virtueson continued. "They think Grandpa may have had a heart attack."

"A heart attack!" Ace burst out with great anxiety, and he suddenly felt a hot, burning sensation begin to creep up the sides of his face and make his hair stand on end. "Is Grandpa all right?" he asked.

"We do not know yet," explained Mr. Virtueson. "An emergency medical team did reach the farm very quickly—considering the traveling conditions tonight—so he and Grandma should be at the hospital soon. The doctors will know what to do when he gets there, but Grandma will need us, and we must go; so please get up and dress right away."

Outside, the wind was screaming and howling fiercely around the eaves of the house. The weather report had predicted a blizzard. Would the ambulance even be able to make it to the hospital?

As that thought plagued him, Ace pulled on his clothes and tied his shoes, but the wild, desperate thoughts raged on in his head. *How could Grandpa have had a heart attack? He certainly looked healthy the last time I saw him, and besides, it is just two and a half weeks before Christmas. Grandpa can't get sick now*, he reasoned to himself . . . *and Dad said it might be a heart attack!*

Grandpa being anything but healthy and strong was a thought that had never crossed his mind, and a sickening feeling churned in the pit of his stomach. What would he do if something really did happen to Grandpa?

Then the howling outside caught his attention again, and for a moment, his thoughts drifted to his beloved pet. The prediction of a blizzard had been the only reason why his father had agreed to bring Wags inside for the night. *I wonder if Wags is making a mess of the laundry room?* He was definitely an outside, not an inside, dog; nevertheless, they could not let him freeze in the snow. The whole situation was a problem, but Ace had no time to think further about Wags, and he quickly finished dressing.

But what about Grandpa? What news awaited them at the hospital? Ace did not dare imagine, and the lump in his throat grew bigger and his heart beat fiercely. Like every child who is close to his grandfather, Ace loved his and could not imagine life without him. Grandpa lived on a farm about a half-hour away, and spending time there was something Ace truly relished. He honestly looked forward to the little chats he and Grandpa had when they shared stories and talked about growing up. Ace's feelings were really mixed up now, and again, all kinds of imaginings raced through his head.

Even though the room had a slight chill, beads of perspiration gathered on Ace's forehead. He was trying to hurry, and yet he wanted to hold back. The sooner he dressed, the sooner they would be on their way to the hospital and the sooner he would know more about Grandpa—that is if the ambulance got there safely on the slippery roads—but did he really want to know? "Emergency" was not a word Ace wanted to face, and yet he realized one phone call could really change a person's life. He had never known his grandfather to be sick—other than maybe just a cold or a little arthritis—and he did not want him to be sick now. Certainly he did not want him to die! Ace sent an urgent plea up to God that Grandpa would get well. "You know how much I need him, Father. I don't want to grow up without a grandpa. You understand, don't You?"

❊ ❊ ❊ ❊

Not too many miles away another boy was uttering a prayer of distress in another situation. "God, we need Your help, and there is no one else." The boy's name was Manny Rodriguez and his family was in trouble. He had never been out in such weather, and winter now had a meaning it never had in Puerto Rico, his homeland. Yes, he had experienced some violent storms—hurricanes to be specific—but never blinding snow and bitter cold. Most of his young life had been spent in the sun near banana plantations with lush tropical forests and the warm ocean not far away. Even at night and in December the family had always slept with the windows open. The cool tropical breezes had been welcome guests for a good night's rest.

Now, here they were, caught in a howling swirl of snow, and it was miserable stuff—cold, wet, and slippery. Worse, their car, which was supposed to carry them to a new, wonderful home, had quit running. Manny's father had pulled to the side of the road and was out in the blizzard with the hood up, trying to get the car started. He was not dressed for such weather; and he had no boots to keep his feet dry nor even a hat to protect his head. Finally, Mr. Rodriguez crawled back into the car and tried the engine. It started with a loud cough, and they all sighed great sighs of relief, for now they could be on their way again. But it was not going to be that easy. Now, the car was stuck in the snow where they had pulled over. Mr. Rodriguez revved the engine. First, he tried pulling forward; then he tried backing up. The tires whirred on the slippery snow and screeched, but the car was stuck, really stuck—no doubt about it.

"You drive, Marilyn," groaned Mr. Rodriguez in frustration as he crawled out into the blinding snow again. "I'll push." Facing the howling blizzard, first he used his bare hands to paw at the snow around the wheels; then he got behind the car and began to push. Manny's mother slid behind the steering wheel and gunned the engine. The car rocked back and forth with the engine roaring, but instead of moving onto the road, the car slid farther and farther to the side into even deeper snow. Next, Mr. Rodriguez moved around to the front of the car. His coat was open and his coal-black hair was flying and falling into his face. In spite of the cold, there were beads of perspiration on his flushed face.

"Okay, Marilyn, let's try backing it out." He bent over, ready to push again; but instead of pushing, he crumpled and collapsed on the hood of the car with an awful groan. Pain showed on his face as he moaned and clutched his chest. Disregarding the snow and cold, both Manny and his mother jumped out to help. They were able to help him back into the car, but now what should they do? They

A man's heart deviseth his way: but the LORD directeth his steps.
Proverbs 16:9

needed help or they would freeze to death right there, alone, in the snow.

"Is it your heart?" asked Manny's mother.

"Maybe," moaned her husband.

Again Manny was praying—praying that his father was not having a heart attack and praying that God would send some help, because there were no friends or relatives nearby to call. Had they been residents of the area, they would have known better than to be out in such a blizzard, but they were strangers to snow and ice and bitter cold weather. They should have been dressed more warmly and taken precautions against the possibility of getting stranded. Mr. Rodriguez moaned again, totally exhausted. In answer to Manny's prayer, at just that moment a vehicle pulled alongside, its motor purring warmly. It was a wonderful, welcome sound, and a kind voice accompanied the gentle knock on the car door window.

"You folks look like you need some help."

CHAPTER 2

SCREECHING SIRENS

The hospital emergency room had been mostly quiet that Wednesday night; then shortly after midnight, the phone started ringing. First, there was a call for the Highland City Hospital ambulance and emergency medical team. They were needed at a farm in the country. This was not welcome news for it was snowing—a real blizzard—and the roads were dangerous. These adverse conditions would certainly make their trip slow and difficult. Even if they got to the patient in time, would they be able to get him back to the hospital for the care he needed?

Right after the first call came another from the small nearby community of Harmony. It had no hospital, but it did have an ambulance and some emergency medical technicians. The call was to alert the doctors and nurses at Highland City Hospital that a patient was en route and that he might have had a heart attack. This was something very serious, and the doctor on duty began giving orders as nurses ran for the emergency "crash" cart. They pulled the device with its oxygen mask, tubes, paddles, and tiny blinking screens into one of the emergency examining rooms. Things were quickly in place, and everything possible would be done to save this patient's life.

Meanwhile, across town, Racer Loyalton heard a siren, then he turned over and saw that the numbers on his alarm clock glowed 1:56 a.m. As an ambulance raced down the street outside, the siren continued its screeching wail, and a quick flash of glaring, yellow light danced across the bedroom curtains. Racer knew it was ambulance lights. He often woke when an ambulance or fire truck went by on nights like this one—nights when his mother worked in the emergency room at the hospital.

Mrs. Loyalton was a dedicated nurse, and she enjoyed her work very much. The same things that made her a great mom also made her a special nurse—she was patient and gentle. She could handle the sight of blood and the strange, medicinal smells of a hospital, which made Racer's head swim; but what she enjoyed most was working with patients who were recovering. They always looked forward to her cheery visits when she brought their medication or came to check their temperature. If they needed something in the middle of the night, she was there to get it, make them comfortable, and then help them get back to sleep. That was what she liked best about nursing; but sometimes, like this snowy night just two and a half weeks before Christmas, she had to take her turn in the emergency room.

Some shifts were very quiet, with just a few cases of bronchitis, upset stomach, or similar complaint. In the small town of Highland City, the ambulance often stayed parked all night. Other times, it seemed one emergency happened after another. Maybe it was a fire in which people had been burned or overcome with smoke; or maybe it was a car accident that resulted in cuts, broken bones, and frightened children. Whatever the circumstances, Nurse Loyalton could be counted on to remain calm; and with quiet efficiency, she would assist the doctors and comfort the hurting.

Racer could still hear the siren in the distance as the ambulance sped to the hospital, and before he fell back to sleep, he wondered who might be on the way there. Maybe it was a sick child or an accident victim. He knew the streets were icy, the wind was howling, and snow had been falling when he went to bed. Such blizzard conditions welcomed all kinds of accidents and strange calamities. Whoever it was, Racer felt certain his mother would be there with the doctors and other nurses to give him or her the best of care. Racer asked the Lord to help his mother to be a special blessing to someone in need. She was usually home in time to fix his breakfast, and sometimes she would share about the people she had helped the night before. Then his father would take him to school. Perhaps in the morning she would tell him all about the reason for the ambulance and its screeching siren.

As he was slipping back to sleep, Racer had a pleasant thought. Maybe he'd wake up to the smell of his mother's hot, fluffy biscuits and gravy. He drifted off to sleep imagining the world's biggest biscuit floating in a lake of gravy, and he was riding in a cereal bowl boat with a spoon for an oar. He rowed and rowed, but he never seemed to get any closer to that fluffy biscuit.

❊ ❊ ❊ ❊

The ambulance from Harmony, with its yellow lights flashing, careened up the icy curving hospital driveway. As the driver braked and hurriedly backed up to the emergency entrance, two EMTs inside the ambulance threw open the rear doors and jumped out. In spite of the cold, a doctor and a nurse rushed out of the hospital through the wide double doors of the emergency entrance to meet the new arrival. Several inches of snow covered the ground, but they did not seem to notice. They were only interested in giving the patient aid and doing it quickly. Another doctor and two nurses, one of which was Nurse Loyalton, waited just inside. She held one of the doors open as the emergency team wheeled the patient briskly past and into the examining room. Everything was happening very quickly, but she did notice that the clock on the wall read 2:05. Then she saw the patient, a man with a dark complexion, perhaps of Hispanic background. He was moaning and looked like he had been exposed to the brutally cold weather. A tube was dangling from one of his arms, and an oxygen mask was over his face. Silently Nurse Loyalton prayed for him and for his family, wherever they were.

The whole emergency room was immediately a hive of activity. Suddenly, a dark-haired woman and a boy, both of whom appeared to be Hispanic, came rushing down the hall. Nurse Loyalton thought the young man looked to be about Racer's age; and the woman, whom Nurse Loyalton took to be the boy's mother and the patient's wife, was shouting. "Let me see my husband! He's having a heart attack! Somebody do something!" She covered her face with her hands and began sobbing.

The two were Manny Rodriguez and his mother. Manny tugged persistently at his mother's coat sleeve and led her to a chair. Although he looked frightened and near tears himself, he quietly said, "Mom, the doctors will help Daddy. He will be okay." Then, as if trying to convince himself, he said, "He has to be okay."

"Oh, God," the sobbing woman pleaded, "please do not let Eduardo die. Please help him. Please help the doctors. Please help us. Please, God, do something." Her whole body was shaking, and her son was pale with concern. He looked first toward the noisy examining room, where his father lay, then back to his mother.

"Nurse Loyalton!" shouted Dr. Harding from the examining room. "We have enough help here. Please go see if you can calm that woman down. If anyone can help her, you can."

Nurse Loyalton quickly did as the doctor requested. He was a good doctor, but he was an unhappy man. Because of some sad circumstances in his life, he had grown bitter. On more than one occasion she had heard him say, "Do not tell me there is a God. A loving God would not let terrible things happen to people." Dr. Harding knew Nurse Loyalton was a Believer because she had shared her faith with him and had told him some of the good things God had done for her family. Even though the doctor did not believe in God, he knew that if anyone could help this sobbing woman who was calling out to God, it was Nurse Loyalton.

CHAPTER 3

COLD RIDE

Mr. Virtueson brought the car around as Ace shut the front door behind him. He could still hear his pet Wags barking from the laundry room. His dog could not understand what was happening, and Ace hoped the barking would not wake their neighbors.

Outside in the bitterly cold, blustery night, Ace looked up into the sky. No moon or stars shone down. It was as black and uninviting as a cave, although pale beams of light did filter down from each tall street lamp, and a cloud of snowflakes whipped and swirled through each soft glow. Probably at least five inches of new snow covered the ground, the sidewalk, and the driveway.

As Ace and his mother hurried to the waiting car, clouds of white poured from its tailpipe and trailed out behind like a coiling snake. The car engine purred loudly. Ace also puffed clouds of white as he sucked in the cold air then breathed it out again. So much had happened in the last half-hour that, to him, it seemed like a dream. First, Dad had wakened him, then he'd been told Grandpa might have had a heart attack, and now they were on their way to the hospital. As they rode along, Ace could hear the snow crunching under the car tires. This meant it was very cold. Neither of his parents spoke as they rode along, being deep in thought and praying for Grandpa. Ace was praying about Grandpa too and thinking.

When Ace and Grandpa had talked on the phone just two days before, they were making plans for the upcoming Christmas holidays; as usual, Ace and his parents were planning to spend several days with Grandpa and Grandma on the farm.

As was the custom, Grandpa and Grandma had been preparing all year for their special way of gift-giving in the community. Two days before Christmas they would hitch Babe, the horse, to the old sleigh and load it down with baskets of food for the needy. Their garden always produced much more than they could eat in a year. Grandpa always slaughtered extra pigs and beef, and Grandma dressed chickens or turkeys so there would be meat as well as canned vegetables and goodies in the baskets.

In the weeks just before Christmas, Grandma—with Grandpa sometimes helping—would bake cookies, fruit cakes, and pies. Everything was lovingly prepared and shared, and this year Grandpa had promised that Ace could ride along in the sleigh in Grandma's place to help make the deliveries. Grandpa said it would save his arthritic knees, and Grandma would not have to go out in the cold and snow. Ace knew there was holly growing in the woods near the farm, and he planned to make some holly wreaths and hang them on the sides of the sleigh.

On Christmas Eve, everyone would go to the little country church for a Christmas Eve service. Afterward, back at the farmhouse, Dad would build a fire in the fireplace; then they would light the Christmas candles, sing Christmas carols, and Grandpa would read the Christmas story out of Luke 2 and Matthew 1. There would be a time of prayer too when they thanked God for all His blessings and prayed for friends and relatives who had never met the Saviour. Eventually, they would drink hot spiced cider, eat Christmas cookies, and talk about other Christmas memories. Finally, when Ace could hardly keep his eyes open, Grandpa would say, "Well, I think it's time to go to bed."

Ace remembered one Christmas when Grandpa had invited the Willings, who were now missionaries to the North Country, to spend Christmas with the Virtueson family. Mr. Willing was Mrs. Virtueson's brother and Ace's uncle. Willie, their son, was about Ace's age. The two of them had had a great time roaming through the big farmhouse, helping Grandpa with barn chores, and talking about their "big" plans for the future. Two years had passed, and now Willie had twin baby brothers named

Hudson and Judson; they all lived far away in the North Country. There would be no friend to pal around with this year. That Christmas with Willie had been a very special Christmas, but this Christmas would be much different.

...O give thanks unto the LORD; for he is good.... Psalm 106:1

CHAPTER 4

IN GOOD HANDS

As Nurse Loyalton guided Eduardo's son and wife to the waiting room, the ambulance was still carefully making its way as quickly as possible through the cold winter night to Highland City Hospital. As the driver slowed for an icy curve, he thought, *What a night to be sick and to need an ambulance.*

In the back of the ambulance, Grandpa Virtueson lay quietly with his eyes closed. A young, fair-skinned, dark-haired EMT calmly checked Grandpa's pulse and blood pressure and tried to reassure him. "You're doing fine. The medicine seems to have helped." His glowing face was bright with hope. "We'll soon be at the hospital and the doctors will be able to find out for certain what is causing your chest pains."

Grandma Virtueson was riding in the ambulance as well. Her gray head was bowed and her hands clasped. Turning to her, the young man gently said, "I believe your prayers have been heard, ma'am. Your husband is doing better. We got to him just in time, and it certainly could have been worse."

"I am very grateful that you came so quickly—especially on such an inclement night," replied Grandma, "and you may call me Grandma Virtueson. Everyone else does."

"Yes, ma'am . . . I mean, Grandma Virtueson. I've done everything I can for your husband for now, but he'll soon be in good hands." He gave her a reassuring smile.

"He is in good hands now," she said confidently.

He assumed she meant him and quickly corrected, "Well, I am not a doctor. When we get to the hospital, Mr. Virtueson, or maybe I should say Grandpa Virtueson, will have a real doctor to take care of him."

"Those are not the 'good hands' to which I was referring," countered Grandma. "I was speaking of the Great Physician, the Lord Jesus Christ. Do you know Him?"

"Yes, I do, ma'am . . . Grandma Virtueson. I haven't known Him long, and I suppose that is why I did not catch your point right away."

A twinkle glinted in Grandma Virtueson's eyes, and in spite of her concern for her husband, a smile teased around the edges of her mouth. She liked this young man whose dark eyes seemed to show hurt and compassion at the same time. "How did you come to trust in the Lord Jesus? What did you say your name is?"

"Keith, Keith Hart. You may not believe this, but I became one of God's children in the emergency room at

Highland City Hospital. This job is one that makes you realize how short life can be and how quickly it can be over." Saying this reminded Keith of where he was and what he was to be doing. Again he attended to Grandpa Virtueson and checked his heart rate and breathing. "How are you doing, sir?"

"Fine, Keith," answered Grandpa softly. "The pain has lessened immensely. Now, tell us your story. It will take my mind off myself and make the trip go faster."

"I never mind sharing my story," said Keith. The Highland City Hospital ambulance bumped and slid its way along the curvy, icy country road. The wind blew, the ambulance sirens blared, but little else disturbed the lonely darkness of the early December morning. Quietly and reverently, Keith Hart shared his story. "Looking back, I can see how God has had His hand on my life all along," he began. "I didn't always feel that way, though."

"God has His hand on every person's life, Keith," added Grandma Virtueson. "It's just that not everyone recognizes that fact. There are many Scriptures that speak of God's knowing us before we were born and of His having a plan and purpose for each one of us. He loved 'the world,' and it is 'not His will that any should perish.'"

"I know that now, but the truth of those facts had not really dawned on me until that night in the emergency room. I was all messed up. I didn't have any real friends, few family ties, and my mother did not understand me. It seemed no one had any answers to my questions and for my problems.

"My childhood was full of painful events, but the one that really shook me up took place when I was only eight years old. My mother became very ill and was diagnosed with bone cancer. It advanced quickly, and . . ." Keith paused for a moment to regain control over his emotions. He continued sadly, "she died. I didn't know how to handle her death. Mother's oldest sister, my Aunt Abigail, took me in and raised me. She was very kind and understanding, but the anger I felt inside came out as disobedience, rebellion, and plain old meanness. I felt totally alone in an unfair world and usually blamed my mother or myself for what had happened. Somehow, in a twisted way, I eventually decided everything must be my fault."

"You know that wasn't correct," commented Grandma. "Keith, you said you went to live with your aunt when your mother died. Where was your father?"

Keith bristled at the mention of his father. "He . . . well, he just wasn't around. I'd rather not talk about that right now." Grandma didn't press him any further, and Keith continued with his story.

"Well, as soon as I was old enough, I joined the army," replied Keith. Just then the ambulance skidded precariously around a sharp curve, and Grandpa groaned. "I'm sorry, Mr. Virtueson. We'll soon be at the hospital. How is the pain?"

"Just the same," Grandpa answered weakly. It had obviously not gone away. "I know there is nothing more you can do. I am in God's good hands, but I am glad you are here. Knowing that a fellow Believer is caring for me is a great comfort. Go on with your story. It is helping, and Mother and I both want to hear it."

Grandma Virtueson reached over and patted Grandpa's hand. Furrows in her brow and creases at the corners of her mouth showed deep concern. "Yes, go on, Keith," she said.

"Well, the army was a whole other chapter of my life. Being so rebellious, I had a rough time taking orders. On the very first day, I did not follow an order exactly, and that did not help my relationship with the drill sergeant. It was only the beginning, and I probably would have ended up being court-martialed if it hadn't been for Dave, my bunk buddy. He was a Believer, a great guy, and the first real friend I had had in a long time. He kept encouraging me to do right and not to be so hard to get along with."

"Did he tell you about the Saviour?" asked Grandma Virtueson.

"Yes, he did. So I started acting better to stay out of trouble. I thought behaving well would get me on the good side of God. I suppose you could say I made a deal with God. I'd be good if He would keep bad things from happening to me. I know now that was wrong. We can't make deals with God. We come to Him in faith and trust Him to work all things together for our good and His glory."

"Amen," whispered Grandpa in a weak voice.

Grandma looked lovingly at her husband, then turned to Keith. "Go on, Keith; how did you get here and become an EMT?"

"In the army I received some medical experience and I liked it; so, when I got out of the army, that was the career I chose. Not long after, I finished my training and began working at Highland City Hospital. I was one of the EMTs at the scene of a bad automobile accident last April. Maybe you remember the one. It happened on Route 12."

"Is that the one in which the little girl was killed?" asked Grandma gravely.

"That's the one," replied Keith sadly. "The girl was eight years old—just the age I was when my mother died. The little girl was hurt very badly—a head injury—and she stopped breathing on the way to the hospital. I was able to revive her, but after she arrived at the emergency room, her heart stopped, and she did not survive. Nothing since the death of my mother had hit me so hard."

Grandma reached over and patted Keith on the shoulder. He choked back the lump in his throat and continued, "Right there in the ER it all became clear. Why had God not taken me when I was eight years old? I knew He must have a purpose for my life. He wanted me to live for Him, not die and miss all the wonderful opportunities He had in store for me. Dave had told me that many times when we were bunking together, but I could not see it then. That night in the ER I understood. So I found a quiet place in the hospital, and right there I asked the Lord Jesus to forgive my sin of rejecting Him. That is when He became my Saviour and best friend."

The ambulance was now speeding down the Highland street leading to the hospital—the street down which Ace and his mother and father had gone minutes before—the street where the Harmony ambulance had traveled less than an hour before. As the wailing of the siren wound down, the Highland Hospital ambulance screeched to a stop and the doors of the ER again opened wide. Grandpa Virtueson was weak and very tired, but just as they had for Mr. Rodriguez, capable hands lifted him and rushed him inside. The trip was over, but the pain was still there. However, hearing Keith talk about his newfound joy and happiness in Jesus Christ gave as much comfort as any medicine.

What lay ahead, Grandpa did not know. Maybe he'd have to face the surgeon's knife. Maybe he'd have to spend Christmas in the hospital recovering. He might even die. But no matter what happened, he knew his life was in God's hands. He prayed that his family would be there, and he was glad he had met Keith.

CHAPTER 5

NEW FRIENDS

Just minutes before the ambulance lurched to a stop outside the emergency room doors, Ace and his mother and father arrived at Highland City Hospital. They heard the siren screeching and then winding down as it came up the hospital driveway. Almost as soon as they reached the waiting room of the ER, Grandma came through the wide double doors. Her face was pale, but she smiled faintly and stretched her arms toward them for strength and assurance. Mr. Virtueson went to her immediately and, putting his strong arm around her, guided her to a chair. When she was seated, Ace hugged her warmly. Grandma squeezed his hands in hers as she always did, and two tears squeezed out of her eyes and rolled down her face. He saw them but only asked anxiously, "How is Grandpa?"

"I am not sure," answered Grandma Virtueson. "He was having chest pains and difficulty breathing when I called your father, but when the emergency medical team got to the farm, they gave him some medication for the pain and oxygen to make his breathing easier. The medication did not take away all the pain, but he was breathing a lot easier and without the oxygen by the time we got here. Keith Hart, the young EMT attending

God is our refuge and strength, a very present help in trouble. Psalm 46:1

Grandpa, seemed very capable, and he is a Believer, which was comforting. He shared his testimony with us during our ride here."

As Grandma was telling all she knew about Grandpa's condition, Ace noticed a boy about his own age across the room. The young man had black wavy hair and a dark complexion. The shirt he wore looked much like the kind Ace wore in summer, and his jacket was thin. He had his arm around a woman, obviously his mother. She was sobbing softly. Fear showed in the boy's dark eyes, but he was trying bravely to comfort his mother.

Ace did not recognize the boy or his mother, but he thought, *I wonder who he is and why he and his mother are here?* Mr. and Mrs. Virtueson and Grandma also noticed the young man and his mother, and Mr. Virtueson suggested to his wife that maybe she should go and see if she could be of some help to them.

Mrs. Virtueson looked at Grandma, wondering if she should leave her, but Grandma patted her on the hand and said, "Go ahead. I am fine. Grandpa is in the Lord's good hands, and those folks look like they need someone to help bear a burden. Ace, you go too. That young man seems to be about your age." She also thought it might get his mind off Grandpa.

Ace and his mother approached the two. "I'm Mrs. Virtueson and this is my son Ace. Is there anything we can do to help?"

The woman choked back tears and hugged her son more tightly. Tears stained both their faces. The mother's eyes were red and puffy. Feeling Mrs. Virtueson's deep concern and compassion, the woman wiped her tears, looked up, and calmly replied, "I'm Marilyn Rodriguez. This is my son Manuel. My husband is ill and we are strangers here."

While Mrs. Virtueson talked with Mrs. Rodriguez and tried to comfort her, Ace struck up a conversation with Manuel. "Do you live around here, Manuel?" he asked politely.

"No," answered the new friend, "and you may call me Manny for short."

"I like that name," replied Ace. "Did your father come in the Harmony ambulance?"

"Yes. He may have had a heart attack."

Ace could sympathize. "The same thing may be true of my grandpa, so I know how you feel. I want you to know both my grandpa and your father are in the Lord's hands."

"Yes, I know," said Manny. "It is not just the possibility of a heart attack that concerns us. That is only part of the problem. My daddy has been out of work, and we were going with him to a new job west of here—a job on a big ranch—when our car quit running. Daddy got the car started, but then we were stuck in the snow. First he tried to drive the car out, but we got stuck worse. When he was trying to push us out, he collapsed." Manny took a quick breath. He seemed to run on in his description, but Ace assumed it was because he was a bit nervous. He determined to try to put Manny at ease and could not help but admire his courage. Meanwhile, Manny continued, "If Mr. Thriftmore from Harmony hadn't come by and helped us by calling an ambulance, Daddy might be dead right now, and Mother and I might be too." He took another quick breath and seemed to relax a little. "It was so cold. I thought for sure we would freeze to death out there."

"This is the biggest snow we have had this winter," commented Ace in a matter-of-fact way. "It seems more like the North Country than Highland City. My cousin Willie Willing wouldn't mind this weather at all. He would think it was great."

"How could anyone think all this snow is great?" questioned Manny in surprise.

"Willie is my cousin, and God has called Willie and his family to be missionaries in the North Country. He and his parents spent Christmas with our family two years ago before they went to the North Country. We had a big snowstorm on Christmas Eve, and Willie thought it was great. He said the cold and snow were God's way of preparing him for his missionary work. Our family and church are praying all the time for the Willings and their work in Spoon Bay and the far-North wilderness areas around there."

"Wow! You have a cousin who is a real live missionary? I can hardly believe it. Since we left Puerto Rico, I've been praying that I would meet another Believer. Now I have met you, and you have a cousin about my age who is a missionary. This is amazing! God is already answering my prayers."

"Yes, and He's going to answer prayer for your father and my grandpa too," added Ace confidently.

For a few moments, Manny forgot the reason why he and Ace had met. There was much he could tell his new friend. Certainly Ace would be excited to know that it was a missionary family who had shared the Gospel with Manny and his family. Manny and his mother had come to know the Lord as a result, but his father had not, and this was another reason why Mrs. Rodriguez and Manny were so concerned.

As the two boys were getting better acquainted, Keith Hart, the EMT, came into the waiting room. He immediately went to Grandma and, kneeling in front of her, he took her hands in his. Ace could hear that he was explaining more about Grandpa's condition and giving her words of encouragement. At one point, she introduced Mr. and Mrs. Virtueson and nodded toward Ace. The young man, who looked to Ace to be in his mid-twenties, rose and came over to the two boys. He stuck out his hand for a friendly handshake, and because he seemed so warm and truly concerned, both responded without hesitation.

"I was in the ambulance with your grandfather, Ace. He is an unusual patient. He certainly has heart attack symptoms, but I feel confident he will get the medical attention he needs and come out just fine."

Then, turning to Manny and pointing toward the examination area, he said, "You must be the son of the other patient in there."

"Yes. My name is Manny Rodriguez." Because he didn't know what else to say, he just started blurting out some facts about himself. "I'm not from around here. Our car is broken down. It is so cold I thought I'd freeze to death. Daddy wants to be a ranch hand. I just met Ace. His cousin is a missionary."

Keith was rather surprised with all this information, but there was no time for a response. Dr. Kerrington, the doctor in charge, entered the waiting room just then, and he had news, but no one knew if it was about Grandpa or about Mr. Rodriguez. Was it good news or bad news? As it turned out, the news was better than expected for both families. Neither Manny's father nor Grandpa Virtueson had truly had a heart attack, although Grandpa Virtueson would need some repair work done on his heart. He would need to recuperate at home for several weeks, but then he should be fine. The doctor said Mr. Rodriguez had just overexerted himself and was exhausted; but he would have to stay in the hospital a night or two for observation.

As Grandpa and Mr. Rodriguez were being officially admitted to the hospital, Ace and Manny passed the time getting better acquainted. "I miss home," admitted Manny. "Puerto Rico has such a warm climate, and I had never seen snow before we came here. How long will this cold weather last?"

"Well, this storm will probably blow itself out tonight," said Ace, "but we will have winter weather for at least two more months. Come March, though, the wildflowers will begin to bloom and things will warm up."

"Like how warm?" asked Manny. To him it seemed cold even in the hospital.

"Oh, in the daytime it will get into the 50s or 60s, maybe even the 70s. You just never know about March. It is almost always windy, perfect kite-flying weather."

"Windy, you say. Have you ever seen a hurricane? Sometimes we get hurricanes back home, but they are very different from this wind that has snow in it. Nothing is the same since we moved here."

Ace decided to change the subject since it seemed only to depress Manny. "Do you have any pets?" he asked.

"No. I had a hamster once, but it ran away. We have moved around a lot, so Daddy thought it was best if I didn't have pets. He says they can sometimes be trouble. How about you? Do you have any pets?"

"Oh, yes," answered Ace. "I have a wonderful dog named Wags, but your father is right when he says pets can cause problems. Take Wags, for instance. He wants to romp and play all the time, and he nearly gets beside himself with excitement each day when I get home from school. He usually jumps around and races back and forth across the yard until he wears himself out. Tonight we had to shut him in the laundry room, though, because it was so cold outside. I hope he is sleeping and not doing any mischief. Dad says the city is not a good place for an active dog like Wags. In warm weather his running around kills the grass; so come spring, we may have to take him out to Grandpa's farm. I think he will be lonely there, though. He needs someone to play with him, and Grandpa does not have time to play with him . . . at least not the way I play with him, and especially since Grandpa will be recuperating."

"Oh, I would love to have a dog, especially one like what you describe Wags to be. He sounds perfect. I would love to run with him and throw balls for him to fetch and teach him tricks and build him a doghouse and help him hide bones and give him baths and brush him down. Whew!" Manny was getting out of breath again. He sighed. "But, I can forget it, at least until Daddy gets a job and we are a lot more settled."

Both boys were thoughtful for a few minutes. Finally, Manny spoke. "Did you say your grandpa has a farm? Is it a ranch? Are there horses and cattle—maybe some longhorns? I've heard about them. My daddy worked on a farm back home for a while. All they raised were cows and goats."

"No, Grandpa's farm is not a ranch. It is just a small dairy farm. Grandpa has all kinds of livestock and poultry, though. It is just enough to keep him from retiring, he says. He loves to plant the crops and see them grow. He enjoys taking care of the animals also. I suppose Dad will have to go out nearly every day now to check on things until Grandpa is back on his feet. Maybe some of the neighbors will help with the livestock while he is in the hospital. Grandpa has helped them many times."

"Yes, well, your grandpa sounds wonderful. I don't have a grandfather. In fact, I don't have any relatives at all except Mother and Daddy—that I know of."

"You're kidding. Everyone has grandparents."

"No, they don't," insisted Manny. "Well, yes, I suppose you would have to say they do or did," he corrected. "I had grandparents, but not now. Mother's parents have already gone to Heaven, and she was an only child. As for Daddy's parents . . . well, he doesn't talk about them much. He told me that his family broke up when he was little. His father, my grandfather, was very troubled as a result of his experiences in war, and his mother felt she had to go live with her relatives. She even took Daddy's little brother with her. My grandfather never got over his depression, and he died when Daddy was just 17. All he has is a picture of himself as a boy with his father. He barely remembers his mother or his brother, and he never heard from them after they moved."

With that Manny shrugged his shoulders and changed the subject. "Let's talk about something else. This all makes me sad. I just want my father to get well now, and I want him to come to know the Lord. This may sound really strange—and I'm not glad Daddy got sick—but I can't think of a better place for it to have happened than right here."

Just then Mr. Virtueson walked up and overheard Manny's comment. "I know God brought us all here tonight for a reason, maybe just so you two boys could meet," he said smiling. "Now, I must take Ace and his mother home, but we will pray for your father before we go. We can praise the Lord that he didn't have a heart attack and also ask Him to work in your father's heart so that he will come to know the Saviour as you and your mother do."

Before they bowed their heads, he added, "By the way, Pastor Gentle from Harmony—where your car broke down—will be here soon. Mr. Thriftmore, the man who stopped to help you and who called the ambulance, is one of Pastor Gentle's church members. The word about your special situation has spread already, and the people of the church insist that you and your mother stay in their 'Hospitality Apartment' until your father is out of the hospital and your family decides where to go from here."

"Really!" exclaimed Manny. He turned to Ace. "Then we might see each other again."

"I would like that very much," said Ace.

CHAPTER 6

NEWS

"Wow, what a storm!" blurted Sandy McMercy as soon as she saw her friend Christi the next morning at Highland School.

"Yes, and did you hear about Ace's grandfather?" Christi added and hurried on. "Pastor called Daddy to tell him what happened. He said Grandma Virtueson had to call 911 early this morning because Grandpa was having chest pains and trouble breathing." She chattered on, not allowing Sandy to say a word. "You know it was serious for them to take him to the hospital in a storm like the one we had last night. He is doing better now, though."

"Wait a minute. Did you say Grandpa Virtueson is in the hospital?" Sandy asked in surprise. "What happened? Where is Ace?"

"Ace is not here," interjected Mr. Friendson, as he came down the hall and heard the girls talking. "He is home getting some rest. From what I have been told, he was at the hospital a good part of the night. I will share everything I know when we get to the Learning Center."

Just then Racer Loyalton, looking very much like an Arctic explorer in his warm parka, came stomping through the front entryway. "**Br-r-r!** The sun may be shining this morning, but it's still cold out there, and the snow is up to my knees."

"Up to your knees?" questioned Christi. For the moment she forgot about Ace and his grandfather. "Why didn't you walk on the sidewalk? Mr. Friendson had it all shoveled when we got here."

"What fun would that be?" countered Racer. "Snow is to play in. Besides, I had to try out my new snow boots."

The girls giggled. It was just like boys to want to get as much snow on themselves as possible. Sandy and Christi liked to sled after a trail had been broken or even play pie tag after someone else had tramped out the pie, but the boys always wanted to roll in the snow or build a fort or dive into snowbanks or at least pummel each other with big, tightly-packed snowballs. If a little went down the back of your neck, that was all the more fun. Christi and Sandy would never understand boys.

Just then the buzzer sounded, letting everyone know school would start in five minutes. More snowy boys pushed through the door, stomping and brushing themselves to get rid of the snow, and they all looked like animated, rosy-cheeked snowmen. "You'd better hurry," suggested Sandy, with a giggle, to Racer, Pudge, Reginald, and Hapford.

A merry heart doeth good like a medicine .... Proverbs 17:22

". . . and you might want to take a quick look in the mirror too," added Christi. None of them seemed to notice that their hair was either going in all directions at once or electrified from pulling off stocking caps. It was truly a sight to behold.

"We're coming," replied Pudge. "You girls missed all the fun."

"Yes, we know," said the girls. They continued giggling as they walked down the hall to the Learning Center.

"I don't know what is so funny," said Pudge to the other boys. "I will never understand girls." Then, turning around as if he had lost something, he said, "Say, where is Ace?"

"Didn't you hear?" began Racer, but then he remembered the time. "Come on; we are going to be late."

"Didn't I hear we are going to be late?" asked Pudge with puzzlement sounding in his voice. None of this was making any sense, but he continued hurrying down the hall with all the others.

"Mr. Friendson will make an announcement in opening exercises, I'm sure," continued Racer. "Grandpa Virtueson is in Highland City Hospital. An ambulance took him there very early this morning."

"What!" exclaimed Pudge. "Why didn't someone tell me sooner?"

"I thought you heard what Mr. Friendson said."

Pudge could not ask any more questions because they had reached the Learning Center. He and Racer just had time to put their schoolwork and supplies in their offices before Mr. Friendson started the opening pledges. Pudge's mouth said the words to the pledges, but his mind was wondering about Grandpa. He was nearly as fond of Ace's grandfather as he was of his own. He had visited the Virtueson farm many times along with several of Ace's other friends. Grandpa and Grandma Virtueson had always made them feel welcome and comfortable, and it was not just because Grandma cooked hearty farm meals. It was much more than that. They were both wise and understanding. This especially meant a lot to Pudge who needed men like Grandpa to talk with since his own father had gone to be with the Lord when Pudge was young.

After the pledges, Mr. Friendson challenged the students with a familiar verse of Scripture. "'And we know that all things work together for good to them that love God, to them who are the called according to his purpose.'" He stopped and looked from face to face. "By now, I am sure most of you have heard that Ace's grandfather is in the hospital. Pastor Alltruth called me early this morning to tell me what had happened and to ask for our prayers. Grandpa Virtueson started having chest pains and shortness of breath last night. The EMTs brought him to the hospital. The pastor has not heard yet what prognosis the doctor has given. Grandpa and the family certainly need our prayers." He continued, "In speaking with Mr. Virtueson early this morning, he asked that we also pray for the Rodriguez family. They were also at the emergency room last night. Mrs. Virtueson and Ace had an opportunity to talk with Mrs. Rodriguez and her son Manuel. Mr. Rodriguez, Manuel's father, collapsed in the snow last night and was taken to the hospital too. The family is from Puerto Rico and they have no relatives here. Their car broke down and probably needs repair work. Mr. Rodriguez was on his way to a new job, but now he may not have a job. Manuel and his mother are Believers, but Mr. Rodriguez does not know the Lord in a personal way. He especially needs our prayers. He certainly needs physical healing, but more important, let's pray that someone will have an opportunity to share the Gospel with him and that he will become a Believer."

"I will pray for Manuel also," Pudge determined quietly.

※ ※ ※ ※

When Pastor Alltruth arrived at Highland City Hospital later that morning, he was directed to Room 120. There he found Grandpa Virtueson resting quietly with Grandma Virtueson by his side. Obviously there was another patient in the room, because the nurses had pulled the curtain around the bed; however, the pastor could not see who it was or how sick he was. Nurses were going in and out checking on both patients, but Nurse Loyalton was not one of them. She was scheduled to work the evening shift.

The pastor greeted and shook hands with Grandma Virtueson, and Grandpa smiled weakly from his bed—the twinkle in his eyes definitely not as bright as usual. At one point, the patient in the other bed groaned, but the pastor did not think it wise to disturb him at the moment. He was really there to visit Grandpa Virtueson; so, presently he would give all his attention to him and Grandma Virtueson. Concerned, but trying to be encouraging at the same time, he asked, "So, what are the doctors telling you about Grandpa's condition, Grandma Virtueson?"

"Well, the good news is that Grandpa did not have a heart attack, but he came very near. If the emergency medical team had not been able to make it through the storm or had not known exactly what to do, there might have been quite a different outcome. It truly was a miracle considering all the circumstances. Part of the miracle is that one of the EMTs who cared for Grandpa is a Believer, and his being there helped us relax and be calm until we reached the hospital. That wasn't easy given the conditions of the roads last night."

"Will Grandpa need surgery?" asked Pastor Alltruth.

"The examination showed that Grandpa has some blockage in one of his arteries. They will do angioplasty. I do not fully understand it, but it seems they insert something similar to a balloon into the artery. When it expands, that clears the artery. He will need some recuperation time, but the doctor feels confident, given Grandpa's otherwise good health, that he should do very well." Grandma looked lovingly at her husband.

He smiled and patted her hand. "Yes, I'll soon be as good as new or even better. Besides, it is not the doctor, but the Great Physician, who is in charge here."

Pastor Alltruth smiled. He understood. "When are they going to do the angioplasty?"

"Tomorrow afternoon," said Grandma.

"Weren't there some warning signs?" asked the pastor.

"There were some signs we both should have recognized but didn't," confessed Grandma. "Grandpa has been tiring out more easily lately. He has even been talking about getting some help with the farm work, but we both thought it was just our age. You know my husband, Pastor. He thinks he is as young as you are."

"Yes, we are both just spring chickens," joked Grandpa. He hadn't lost his sense of humor. Pastor Alltruth inwardly chuckled. Compared to Grandpa, he might be young, but to some others, namely Racer, Pudge, Ace, Christi, Sandy, and several young people around the church, his gray hair made him nearly as old as Methuselah—but they also thought it made him wise.

With that sobering thought, Pastor Alltruth changed the subject. He spoke to Grandpa. "You know I will be here tomorrow to check on you after they do the angioplasty. Now let's have a word of prayer."

"Would you include me and my family in that prayer, Pastor?" came a tired voice from the bed behind the curtain.

"Of course," replied Pastor Alltruth. He pulled back the curtain.

Grandma Virtueson quickly explained, "Pastor, this is Eduardo Rodriguez. He was brought to the hospital last night also."

"And what are the doctors telling you, Eduardo?" asked the pastor with genuine concern in his voice.

"Just that I overexerted myself and need rest. I collapsed in the snow last night when I was trying to push our car out of a drift. It is all very discouraging and unfair. I need to get to a job; so . . . I'm asking you to pray that

I will feel well enough to leave the hospital tomorrow. I need to get my car fixed too. Last night a church in Harmony put up my wife and son, but I won't continue to accept their charity. All I need is for God to give me some help. Is that too much to ask?"

"I certainly do want to pray about all this, Eduardo, but let me ask you something else. Are you a Believer?"

"My wife and boy are. They go to church all the time . . . and I go once in a while."

"Attending church is certainly important, Eduardo, but I'm asking you if you have a personal relationship with Jesus Christ."

"I know what you are talking about, Pastor, but I am not ready to go that far yet. I need to get some things worked out first." He sighed deeply. "Don't you understand? If I can just get out of this hospital and get back to work, I can take care of my family. I've always managed to do it before. Maybe when I get things back under control, I'll have time for what you are talking about. Please stay out of my personal life and just pray that I will get well."

"As you wish," replied Pastor Alltruth calmly. He took both Grandpa's hand and Mr. Rodriguez's hand. Quietly and earnestly he prayed for Grandpa and for Mr. Rodriguez and his family.

Hearing the Pastor's calm, beseeching voice lifted to the Heavenly Father was a great comfort to Grandma and Grandpa. To Mr. Rodriguez that was not the case, however. Instead of feeling better, it seemed the emptiness he felt inside grew even greater, and he tried to put it aside.

After Pastor Alltruth finished praying, he silently lifted another concern to his Heavenly Father. He prayed that Mr. Rodriguez would realize his urgent need for the Saviour—the only One who could rescue him from sin and teach him how to truly care for his family. Since Mr. Rodriguez was not a Believer, he did not understand that he could not work things out by himself; nor could he do what was best for his wife and son. Pastor Alltruth knew that Mr. Rodriguez's only hope was to put aside his pride and seek God's forgiveness.

CHAPTER 7

DETECTIVE ON THE LOOSE

While Ace's friends were going through their regular school routine and Pastor Alltruth was visiting Grandpa in the hospital, Ace was sound asleep, catching up on the rest he had missed the night before. He slept peacefully because, before he laid his head on the pillow, he had thanked the Lord for the wonderful comfort of God's Word. Even before he had gotten to the hospital, God's Spirit had reminded him of a precious promise—the one found in Philippians 4:6,7. "Be careful [anxious or worried] for nothing; but in every thing by prayer and supplication with thanksgiving let your requests be made known unto God. And the peace of God, which passeth all understanding, shall keep your hearts and minds through Christ Jesus."

Claiming that promise had settled Ace's fears and doubts. He did not have to be concerned over Grandpa's condition because God was in control, and he did not have to be selfish and think only of himself and how he would feel if something happened to Grandpa. Instead he could allow God to use this situation for His glory. Later, he had seen one way in which God did just that when he was able to share the same Scripture with Manny, his new friend.

By late morning, Ace was rested and fully awake. He reviewed all that had happened much earlier that morning. Yes, Grandpa had had a near heart attack and had been taken to the hospital. At the hospital, Ace had met a new friend. This new friend did not have the wonderful advantages he had, and Ace tried to imagine what it would be like not to have a permanent home, to know uncertainties lay ahead, and to have a father with whom he could not share spiritual concerns. Manny was a boy just like he was, and boys sometimes have special things they need to talk about, and they need a spiritual male role model. That was what Ace appreciated so much about his own father, his grandpa, his pastor, and even his uncle, Mr. Willing. Poor Manny, though, did not have any spiritual male figure in his life. His mother knew the Lord, and Ace was sure she did all she could to fill the gap, but Ace knew there were some things Manny could not share even with her, because she was not a man. His heart went out to his new friend. *I am so blessed*, he thought.

When Manny had shared his uncertain feelings, it had bothered Ace very much. Neither could he forget the sad look on Manny's face when he had said, "I don't have a grandfather. In fact, I don't have any relatives at all—that I know of." He had declared that he lacked the security of an extended family, although he desperately wanted one.

Particularly the *I don't have any relatives—that I know of* had struck Ace and puzzled him. It was almost as if Manny were leaving room for doubt—that maybe deep down he held out some hope that other family members might exist. Perhaps there was even a male relative who could be a spiritual leader for Manny. He had confirmed that his grandmother had gone to live with relatives. Was it possible that some of them were still living? Manny's father seemed to have no desire to find them, if they existed, but that didn't mean there weren't any. Maybe Manny's grandmother and uncle were still alive. Ace thought it was time to find out, and he thought he knew where he could get some help. It would be like "looking for a needle in a haystack" as Grandpa would say, but wasn't it worth a try, to help his new friend?

As he showered and dressed and had brunch with his mother, he thought about his idea some more. Should he tell Manny what he was planning? Would Manny really want to find his relatives? Would Manny's father be against it? He had better talk with Manny before he initiated any detective work.

CHAPTER 8

GOD OF THE IMPOSSIBLE

Ace, his parents, Grandma Virtueson, and Pastor Alltruth were at the hospital the next afternoon, waiting while Grandpa underwent the angioplasty procedure. Not long after Grandpa had been whisked into surgery, Keith Hart showed up, and Mr. Virtueson introduced him to Pastor Alltruth, sharing briefly why Keith was so interested in Grandpa's condition.

"When Grandpa gets to feeling better, you should go out to the farm some day," suggested Ace. "He would love to show you around."

"By all means," said Grandma Virtueson, "you would be welcome anytime."

"Thank you for the invitation. I would like that very much," said Keith, and then he changed the subject. "By the way, what happened to the Rodriguez family? I thought Manny seemed like a very nice young man. I thought he was going to tell me his whole life history in one breath!"

Since Ace had spent quite a while talking with Manny in the emergency waiting room the night before last, he was able to bring Keith up to date. "Mr. Rodriguez doesn't have a job, their car needs repairs, and they have no relatives around here to help them out," explained Ace. Keith quickly recognized that Ace was concerned about his new friend.

Keith wanted to visit another patient he had brought to the hospital the night before, so he finished his conversation with Ace and told everyone he would return to visit Grandpa after his surgery. As he walked down the hall, he thought, *I am so blessed to have met the Virtuesons!* He had come to really appreciate the fellowship with his new friends, especially Grandpa. Keith had witnessed Grandpa's faith in action that night in the ambulance, and it had made quite an impression on the young EMT. He had found in Grandpa a source of spiritual guidance and wisdom that he desperately needed, and he intended to spend as much time with Grandpa as possible.

After Keith left, Pastor Alltruth reflected on what Ace had said about the Rodriguez's troubles. He immediately spoke up. "I know our people at church will want to do all they can to help."

To everyone's surprise, just then, down the hall came Manny, his mother, and Mr. and Mrs. Thriftmore. Ace's new friend waved and came into the waiting room.

"Hi," he said, addressing Ace. "How is your grandpa?"

Ace explained that they were waiting and praying that the angioplasty would be successful, but they all wanted to know from Manny when the doctor was going to release Mr. Rodriguez.

"We are here to pick him up now," said Manny happily. "Dr. Harding, Dad's doctor, says he can leave if he promises not to try to push any more cars out of the snow." Then he hurried on with more good news. "You won't believe all that has happened since I saw you last. Not only have the people of Harmony Chapel said we can stay in their 'Hospitality Apartment' as long as we need to, but today, because I was there, I visited Harmony School. Guess what? Pastor Gentle and Mr. Trueword said I can go to school every day until we leave." His dark eyes were dancing as he continued excitedly, "Ace, I have always wanted to go to a school like Harmony School. I met Booker Thriftmore and some of his friends. They are like you. They make me feel welcome. I could live here forever."

"Why not?" asked Ace. "Would your parents agree?"

Manny's happy expression quickly faded. "No, Daddy says when the car is fixed, if the ranch hand job is still available, we are leaving. He doesn't want our family to keep 'bumming' from other people."

Just then Mr. Thriftmore spoke up; his eyebrows pinched in dismay. "Now wait a minute. You folks are not 'bumming' from anyone. I told your father I would help him fix his car. I believe there must be water in the fuel line because of the snow and sudden changes in temperature. I will show him what to do, but he will have to do the work himself. As for staying in the 'Hospitality Apartment,' that is why the folks at our church prepared it—to reach out in hospitality. The Bible commands us to do so."

"Does it?" queried Manny.

"Yes, in Romans 12:9 and 13. 'Let love be without dissimulation [hypocrisy] . . . Distributing to the necessity of saints; given to hospitality.' You are giving us an opportunity to show hospitality and Christian charity. We haven't had the opportunity in a while. Besides, who knows, God may have a job waiting for your father right here in Highland City or Harmony. He certainly had some reason for bringing you here."

"Hm-m," responded Manny thoughtfully. "I could agree, but you may have to convince my father. He still insists we aren't settling here. He wants to be a cowboy and work on a ranch."

"Well, for now at least, it looks like God wants you here," chimed in Ace, "because He is providing a place for you to stay, and He is meeting your needs."

"And I believe God will give your dad a job right here in this area, maybe even today," said Mr. Thriftmore.

"Impossible!" retorted Manny. "I can't believe that could happen too."

"Oh, really?" said Mr. Thriftmore, pointing his forefinger upward. "Did you forget? Our God is the God of the impossible."

". . . and of the practical," added Mr. Virtueson. He had just gotten a fantastic idea. "Fellows, I do not know for certain that Grandpa will agree, but I have an idea. Maybe Mr. Rodriguez can be a ranch hand of sorts right here near both Harmony and Highland City."

"How?" asked both boys with enthusiasm.

"Think about this." He leaned forward, and the boys listened eagerly. "Who is going to take care of the livestock and watch over the farm while Dad is recuperating? It is not realistic for me to think of going out to the farm twice a day to milk the cows and feed and care for the other animals. Manny, I heard you tell Ace the other night that your father has done farm work."

"He has—in Puerto Rico," replied Manny.

"It is not so different here. We have the same animals, and I can give him pointers for the special feed and care farm animals need in winter. Cows and goats still have to be milked twice a day, and the eggs still have to be gathered—just to mention a few chores."

"Wow, do you think it could really work out?" asked Manny, glancing from Mr. Virtueson to Ace, who was smiling enthusiastically. Grandma was smiling as well, and she seemed especially happy at the possibility.

Mr. Virtueson saw Grandma's pleased look and asked, "What do you think, Mother? It might solve two problems."

"I think it could be an answer to my prayer, son; of course, your father must give his approval."

Mr. Virtueson agreed to talk with Grandpa; then the Thriftmores, Manny, and his mother started down the hall to see if Mr. Rodriguez was ready to leave.

Before Manny had gone far, Ace caught up to him and whispered mysteriously, "I have something else to talk about with you soon, something that will require your parents' permission."

While Pastor Alltruth and the Virtueson family waited for a report on Grandpa, the nurses, doctors, and other hospital personnel went about their duties. From his chair in the waiting room, Ace watched them bustle by. Some had carts of clean bed linens, some had charts and medication in hand, and still others pushed huge meal carts stacked full of empty trays from lunch. There were also workers with mops and cleaning supplies. He guessed that was why hospitals always had an antiseptic smell.

Eventually, he saw a nurse wheel Mr. Rodriguez past and down the hall to be discharged. The Thriftmores, Mrs. Rodriguez, and Manny trailed along behind. As they passed the windows separating the hall from the waiting room, Manny waved. Ace saw he was beaming with anticipation. The expression on his face seemed to say, "How can I help but be happy? All the sad days seem to be behind, and only good days are ahead. Daddy did **not** have a heart attack after all, the car **can be** fixed, and Grandpa Virtueson is probably going to hire Daddy as a farmhand. But, best of all, I will be close to my new friends in Harmony and be able to see Ace often."

Yes, the days ahead definitely looked bright, and Manny was surprised that God had worked things out so soon and so wonderfully. Only one thing still hung like a cloud overhead to dampen his spirits. His father did not share a love for the Lord, and the recent hardships had only served to make him more bitter. "Why can't God let things go my way for once," his father would say, "since He is supposed to be in control?" Manny wondered what it would take to break down the wall of bitterness his father just kept building higher, and it didn't help any when, as the discharge papers were being completed, Dr. Harding released a stream of grievous remarks.

"I saw you were in the same room as Grandpa Virtueson," he grouched. "He is quite a case, isn't he? The whole family is disgusting. They all try to be so goody-goody and force their 'the Bible says' stuff down one's throat. I have to deal with Nurse Loyalton all the time; she is one of those 'Believers,' you know. I hope you did not let Grandpa get to you."

"He is okay," answered Mr. Rodriguez. At the moment he was not in the mood to talk about his feelings.

"Well," Dr. Harding continued sourly, "all I can say is, if God were so loving, why would He take a man's family away from him, as He did mine?" His sad, empty eyes grew shiny as a hint of tears began to gather, but he quickly squeezed them back. "I will never forgive God for that. First, He took my baby; then He took my wife. Sometimes the pain is so great, I just don't think I can bear it."

Mr. Rodriguez acknowledged what Dr. Harding said. "Losing one's family is hard to accept," he said. His mind flashed quickly over the loneliness he had experienced in his childhood and before he met Marilyn, his wife. There was bitterness in his heart as well, and more than once he, too, had felt anger toward God. But now he had his wife and Manny, and he was not going to let God or anything else hurt them or come between them. "Nothing means more to me than my wife and son," he said, as much to himself as to the doctor.

Just then an office worker came with the completed paperwork and placed it in front of Mr. Rodriguez. "Just sign here."

Dr. Harding shook Mr. Rodriguez's hand and said grimly, "You are discharged, and I doubt I will need to see you again. I hope things turn out better for you than they have for me."

Manny took that to mean Dr. Harding did not expect his father to have any more physical problems. As it turned out, though, Dr. Harding's comment was very prophetic.

CHAPTER 9

A GOOD REPORT

Finally, just past 4 o'clock, Dr. Kerrington, Grandpa's physician, brought news about Grandpa. Keith walked up just as the doctor began speaking. "The angioplasty went fine. Aside from the blockage, which the angioplasty has successfully corrected, Grandpa Virtueson has a very strong heart. He is in good health for a man his age. We will keep him here for a few days; then, if he promises to rest at home, we will discharge him. I expect an uneventful and complete recovery. When the new year rolls around, he should be able to take on some light chores—nothing very strenuous though."

"Praise the Lord!" shouted Ace. He was so thankful that Grandpa would soon be well and especially that he would soon be home. Maybe they could have a truly traditional Virtueson Christmas after all.

Just then, Dr. Harding came around a corner and heard what Ace said as he walked by.

"Humph!" he grunted in Ace's direction. Ace wondered what had disturbed the doctor.

Dr. Kerrington, however, had a different response. "I praise the Lord as well," he said. He had overheard Dr. Harding and sighed, shaking his head. "It is sad that not all doctors realize their patients' lives are really in the Great Physician's hands and not in their hands." His gaze followed Dr. Harding; then he turned and spoke to those in the room. "If you don't stay long, I believe Grandpa might be ready for some visitors, and I don't see any reason why you can't come also, Keith."

When the Virtuesons and Keith got to Grandpa's room, he was alone and resting quietly.

"How are you, Grandpa?" asked Ace.

"Better, much better," replied Grandpa. "I can hardly believe such a simple thing as inserting a balloon into my artery could make so much difference. Doctor Kerrington says I still have to take it easy and not do any farm work until after New Year's, and then only light chores."

"I'm glad you brought that up," said Ace. "Dad has a wonderful idea."

"Oh?" asked Grandpa, raising himself just a little.

"Yes," Ace answered excitedly. "He thinks you should hire Mr. Rodriguez as a farmhand and let him take care of all the chores around the farm until you are fully recovered and ready to take over the farm work again."

"Hm-m," mused Grandpa. He had to think about that. Finally, turning to Grandma, he asked, "What do you think, Dear?"

"We talked about it while you were having the procedure done. This really may be God's way of working things out. He knew you were going to get sick and would need help on the farm while you were recuperating. He also knew about the needs of the Rodriguez family. Perhaps their getting stranded in Harmony and our meeting them was God's way of providing someone to take care of the farm until you are well again."

Ace had another thought to add. "Maybe it is also God's way of answering some prayers for Manny. He wants to meet some other young people and go to a Christian school. He is also praying that his father will come to know the Lord. Grandpa, if he were around you and Grandma, you would have opportunities to talk with him. Maybe you could convince him to become a Believer."

"Whoa, wait a minute, Ace. I agree that God certainly knew our paths would cross with the Rodriguez family, but He doesn't move people around like checkers on a checkerboard. Furthermore, when Mr. Rodriguez comes to know the Lord—and I am confident he will—it won't be because I am able to persuade him. The Lord will have to soften his heart."

"I agree, Grandpa," sighed Ace. "I just meant that perhaps, if Mr. Rodriguez could see Christian love in action around him, he might want what we have."

"Okay, just so there is no misunderstanding. Now about the farmhand job—the Rodriguez family will also need a place to live. What about that?"

"Right now they are staying in the 'Hospitality Apartment' at Harmony Chapel," said Ace, "and they can stay as long as they need to. Manny said so."

That comment brought a response from Grandma. "The folks at Harmony Chapel are being very hospitable; but the Rodriguezes cannot stay there forever, and they would need to be close at hand. Dear," she said in her sweetest persuasive tone, "we have several empty bedrooms, and I wouldn't mind an extra set of hands around the house, especially with Christmas coming and you recuperating."

"I guess I do help with a lot of little things around the house during the Christmas holidays, don't I?" reasoned Grandpa. "I always put up the lights outside, hang wreaths in the windows, and even help you with baking."

"Yes, but not this year. So, as you see, I really could use some help."

Ace brought up another concern. "And what about delivering the food baskets to the needy? You said I could go with you this year."

"Well, I suppose your father will have to drive the sleigh this year. He knows how to handle it and Babe. Also, the Rodriguezes' son . . . What is his name?"

"Manny," answered Ace.

"Well, I suppose Manny could probably ride along too and help you carry the food baskets to the doors. How would that suit you?"

"Fantastic!" exclaimed Ace, slapping his thighs. "We can still have a Virtueson Christmas."

"Then it is settled," stated Grandpa. "Son, talk with Mr. Rodriguez and see if he will take the job. If he is agreeable, the family can move out to the farm this weekend, and I'll be home next week—I trust."

Keith had been silently standing by listening to the conversation. Later, when the conversation lagged, he spoke up. "Ace suggested that I come out to your farm and visit you. Would you mind?"

"Not in the least," replied Grandpa. "Hopefully, Mr. Rodriguez will take us up on our offer, and you can spend some time with Manny."

"I would like that very much," replied Keith.

"Splendid," declared Grandpa. "I'll expect to see you soon—and not in the back of an ambulance."

CHAPTER 10

A CHALLENGING OPPORTUNITY

Friday afternoon, as soon as school was out, Mr. Virtueson picked up Ace, and they headed toward Harmony to talk with Mr. Rodriguez. Ace was glad his father had waited so that he could go along. He needed to see Manny as soon as possible because he had some very important news to share with him. Then his thoughts turned to Grandpa.

"You visited Grandpa today, didn't you?" he asked his father.

Mr. Virtueson nodded affirmatively. "He is doing fine and wants to get home. Dr. Kerrington says he must stay until Monday, but then if everything is okay, he may go home."

"Was Grandma there too?"

"Yes, and she was making all kinds of plans. I certainly hope Mr. Rodriguez takes the job. Mother has her heart set on their moving out to the farm. I believe it is more than just having some help. I think she would really enjoy having another woman in the house for awhile. When I took her home earlier this afternoon, she was talking about how she will rearrange the extra rooms to make the

Rodriguezes feel at home. If they were to turn down the offer now, I'm afraid she would be very disappointed."

"I don't see how Mr. Rodriguez can turn it down, do you?" asked Ace. "The family will have a small income—which is more than they have now—and they will get to live in a real house and have all the food they want to eat." He continued with confidence, "Of course he will take it."

Mr. Virtueson tilted his head and gave a doubtful nod. "Do not be so sure, Ace. Mr. Rodriguez is a proud, self-sufficient man who wants to think he can work things out without help from other people."

". . . or God," added Ace quickly.

"That's true," agreed his father. "I would not advise making any big plans just yet. We have to leave all this in the Lord's hands."

At just that moment, Mr. Virtueson turned onto the street where Harmony Chapel was located, and they could see the church. Mr. Rodriguez was working on his car in a lean-to shed at the side of the building. The hood was up and a toolbox was sitting on the ground. As the Virtuesons drove up, he pulled his head out from under the hood and stood up.

Ace and his father hopped out of the car and went over to him. Mr. Rodriguez turned and grabbed a rag to wipe his greasy hands. Ace thought the car was probably fixed, and Mr. Rodriguez must surely be in a good mood. Mr. Rodriguez greeted them cordially, but in a distant manner. He pointed in the direction of the "Hospitality Apartment" and said to Ace, "You probably want to go inside and see Manny. He is doing schoolwork." Then he added in a half grunt, "That has to be a first—his liking schoolwork."

Ace gladly went inside. He could hardly wait to share his big news with Manny. The two boys greeted each other and exchanged school news; then Ace could wait no longer. "Manny, I have some super news since I talked with my friend Reginald Upright today. How would you like to find out if you have any other relatives?" He did not wait for a response from Manny but went on excitedly, "I have felt so sad since you told me that you have no grandfather. I cannot imagine how lonely you must feel at times. I just think there is something we can do about that." He paused just for a moment before finishing. "You told me that your grandfather died in Puerto Rico, but that your grandmother went to live with her relatives. Isn't it possible that some are still living . . . somewhere? Maybe you have aunts or uncles or cousins? Wouldn't you like to find them? Then you would have an extended family."

The response Ace received was not what he was expecting. Manny almost seemed disappointed in his new friend. "Don't you think I have thought about that many times? But it is hopeless," he said. "I have accepted that Mother and Daddy are the only relatives I have." He paused and hung his head dejectedly. "Besides, there is no way to find out, is there?"

Right away Ace heard the glimmer of hope in Manny's voice and knew he did have some interest. He was not going to give up so easily. "Reginald says it can be done. He wants to help and even said he would find it 'a very challenging opportunity.' He is sure he can find out something about your grandmother's past and any living family members. We just need your parents' permission and a little family information."

"How could Reginald do that—I mean find someone's relatives?" asked Manny.

"Reginald would use his computer. He says it would not be that hard. He knows all about how to get information, and his father has done a lot of research into their family's genealogy, so he could help also. What do you think?" Ace was excited. He thought it was the best idea he had had in some time, and he wanted to help Manny know more about his heritage and have an extended family as he did. He could not imagine his new friend would not be excited at the prospect.

"And what if Reginald finds out what I already feel is certain?" asked Manny not wanting to open himself up to disappointment. "I do not have any relatives except Mother and Daddy, so why should I get my hopes up just to have them dashed?"

"I think you are already hoping a little bit," said Ace encouragingly, "but you are afraid to admit it. Now come on, let's go ask your mother first."

Mrs. Rodriguez was immediately sympathetic. She understood that her son wanted to feel that he had family beyond just she and her husband. She was curious too but had never thought it was possible to trace Manny's heritage. Now, here was a way, and she encouraged him. She was willing to help and gave her permission.

Finally, Manny began to seem a little excited over the idea. Maybe there was someone out there—a family, a heritage to which he belonged. Visions of family reunions with aunts and uncles and oodles of cousins began to flood his imagination. There may not be any grandparents, but if he had aunts and uncles and cousins, that would be enough. Ace's idea was a good one after all.

Then the two boys threw on their coats and ran out to the lean-to shed excitedly. "Daddy, guess what," exclaimed

Manny. "Ace has a friend who can use the computer to find out about our relatives. All he needs is a little information from you and your permission to search. You will give your permission, won't you?"

Ace began to explain what Reginald could do through the computer, but Mr. Rodriguez's face flushed as he squeezed his fists and set his jaw. Manny was not used to seeing his father react this way, and it surprised and frightened him. What had he or Ace said that should upset his father so?

"No, absolutely not," said Mr. Rodriguez firmly. "If we have relatives, I do not want to see them, and they would probably not want to see me either. I have nothing to feel good about in my background, so forget this foolishness. I certainly will **not** give my permission, and I do not want to hear another word about it."

He had flatly settled it, so there was not going to be any detective work done. Both Manny and Ace were crushed. It had not turned out at all as Ace had envisioned, and he felt responsible for Manny's hopes being dashed.

As they drove back home in the car, Ace forgot about the offer Mr. Virtueson had come to make to Mr. Rodriguez. He was too taken up in his own thoughts of disappointment. Finally, Mr. Virtueson asked what was wrong, and Ace told him all about it.

His father tried to be sympathetic and said, "I do not believe we can understand the pain and guilt and anger Mr. Rodriguez has been carrying around for years."

"But he needs to think of people other than himself," declared Ace.

"Maybe so," said his father, "but we cannot really understand how he feels, and we certainly cannot change his mind."

"Well, he did take Grandpa up on his offer to run the farm, didn't he?" asked Ace, with full assurance that at least part of the plan would come about. "Then at least Manny and I can still see each other and be friends."

"I am sorry to tell you this, but he turned it down," said Mr. Virtueson. "He still has his mind set on being a ranch hand, but somehow I think it has more to do with his pride. I did tell him he could change his mind and to call if he did. I gave him all the details and told him that we needed him as soon as possible."

Both Ace and his father were sad they did not have better news when they got home. Ace told his mother about his wonderful idea to find some relatives for Manny and how it had backfired. She assured him it had been a kind, thoughtful idea, but added, "Some hurts are very deep, and Mr. Rodriguez has not turned his over to the Lord." Mr. Virtueson was not certain, either, how he would tell Grandpa and Grandma they still needed to find a farmhand. He hoped it would not set Grandpa back in his recovery.

CHAPTER 11

WORK TO DO

Saturday morning dawned clear and crisp, but Ace and his father and mother had been up before the sun. There had been another light snow during the night, but the weather report promised a sunny day. Things looked brighter over hot biscuits and eggs, and Ace decided he must leave the problem of Manny's not having any relatives up to the Lord. As the family talked, Mr. Virtueson said, "I have an idea, Ace. Tell me what you think."

Ace nodded affirmatively to show he was listening, but he couldn't say anything because his mouth was full of biscuits and eggs.

"Since Mr. Rodriguez turned down Grandpa's offer to move out to the farm, I need to go out there today and try to work out something with the neighbors to get the chores done each day. Your mother would like to go too. You see, when I called Grandma last night to tell her that the Rodriguezes would not be moving to the farm, she was very disappointed. She was so looking forward to Mrs. Rodriguez's company and help with the holiday cleaning, decorating, and food baskets. So, your mother is going to help her as much as she can today. We will probably be there until late afternoon. We will take Wags along, but I thought you still might get bored. What would you think about taking Pudge and Hapford and Racer along? You fellows can go sledding and play in the snow after we do a few chores."

Ace had been rather glum after the disappointing news of the night before, but now he brightened. "May I invite Reginald as well?" A pleading look crossed his face.

"I suppose that would be fine. Is there anyone or anything else you would like to bring along?" he asked jokingly.

But Ace took him seriously. "If Mother is going to help Grandma do housecleaning, put out Christmas decorations, and maybe start baking for the food baskets, couldn't Christi and Sandy come along to help? Maybe they could bake some cookies for us. I know Pudge and Racer would like that."

"Oh," laughed Mr. Virtueson, giving Ace a sly look, "as if you wouldn't." Ace just grinned and turned a little pink. Dad understood him very well. Then Mr. Virtueson continued, "It is doubtful everyone can go on such short notice, but if you do some hasty calling and they have permission to go, I'll borrow the church van and we will take everyone. A break in routine would be good for all of us, I suppose. It has been a rather stress-filled few days.

Before we pick up your friends, though, we will make a quick stop at the hospital to see Grandpa and take any messages he has for Grandma."

"Yeah!" cheered Ace, cramming the last crumbs of biscuit into his mouth and hurriedly carrying his dirty plate and silverware to the sink. Then he headed for the telephone to call his friends from Highland School. While he did that, Mother finished cleaning the kitchen, and Dad fed Wags and got his carrying cage ready.

If Mr. Virtueson had not known better, he would have thought Wags had been listening to the breakfast-table conversation. The frisky dog wagged his tail and jumped and ran excitedly around the yard as if he knew a fun time was about to begin. The whole family loved him, but he was really Ace's pet.

Mr. Virtueson had let Ace pick him out at a pet store when Ace was about six years old, and since that time, little had kept them apart for long. Having a pet had been good for young Ace because it had taught him to treat animals with respect, and Wags had become the little boy's protector.

Now, Ace and Wags were both bigger. Ace had assumed more responsibilities around the house and church, and Wags seemed to like being at the farm better than in the yard. Maybe he anticipated an adventure that would give him more room to explore and frolic.

As Mr. Virtueson stepped back into the house, Ace nearly bowled him over. "Everyone can go!" he shouted. "Reginald's father had planned to take him to some kind of exhibit, but when I called, his father decided fresh air and exercise would be good for him." I told each of them we would pick them up sometime between 10:00 and 10:30, after we stop at the hospital. Does that fit into our plans?"

"That sounds splendid. Let me get my old clothes and a few tools that I want to take along. Please check to see if your mother needs any help with cleaning supplies, and be sure you wear your warmest coat, but not your best one. Take some extra socks and gloves too. You know how easily they get wet in the snow, and an extra hat would do well also."

Nearly before Ace knew it, they had everything ready and were heading for the hospital to see Grandpa, and on the way, they stopped to pick up the church van. The city road crews had cleared the streets earlier that morning, and the sun was shining bright and warm. It would be a perfect day for sledding and playing in the snow.

Ace was very impressed when they arrived at Grandpa's hospital room. Balloons and flowers and cards filled the one big windowsill and both night tables. And

O taste and see that the Lord is good: blessed is the man that trusteth in him. Psalm 34:8

Grandpa! Ace could hardly believe how well he looked just three days after almost having a heart attack. His face glowed with vitality, and he was sitting up in bed, having already had his morning walk up and down the hospital halls. It was a small hospital, so he hadn't walked far, and Nurse Loyalton had walked with him.

"Doctor Kerrington says walking a little every day is the best thing I can do to get my full strength back," explained Grandpa.

Earlier, Mr. Virtueson had decided that unless Grandpa asked, they would not tell him yet that Mr. Rodriguez had turned down the job as farmhand because it might set back his recuperation. Ace was still thinking about the wisdom of that decision as Grandpa held up each get well card and explained who had sent it. He seemed so pleased and relaxed. The balloons and flowers held special significance to him, and were further confirmation of his positive influence on so many lives.

Suddenly, Mr. Virtueson's cell phone rang. They were all a little startled. It didn't ring often, but Mr. Virtueson always carried it in case the pastor or someone else needed to reach him.

"Hello," he said, followed by a cautious, "Yes, Mr. Rodriguez."

Ace immediately perked up and wondered what was going on in Manny's life now. His new friend had been in high spirits after his father had left the hospital. He had been so happy and encouraged; the world had looked bright and rosy, but it had not lasted long. That very day when Ace and his father had visited, Manny had experienced two crushing disappointments. First, his father had refused to give permission for Reginald to do the computer detective work; then he found out his father had not accepted Grandpa Virtueson's offer to move to the farm. Ace was disappointed too, but he knew it must have been even more discouraging for Manny, and he hoped the phone call would not announce more bad news for his friend.

"Great! Wonderful!" Mr. Virtueson was exclaiming, still holding the phone to his ear.

What? What? Ace's face was saying to his father. Mr. Virtueson gave a thumbs-up sign as he continued to listen to what Mr. Rodriguez was saying; so Ace knew it surely had to be good news. As Mr. Virtueson hung up, he was smiling.

"Well, everyone," he announced with a deep sigh of joy and relief, "we now have a farmhand to take over the farm work while Dad recuperates."

"Yes!" exclaimed Ace dramatically. He was elated. This meant Manny would not be leaving, and maybe Mr. Rodriguez would eventually change his mind and allow Reginald to search for Manny's other relatives. Ace so wanted Manny to have an extended, supportive family as he did.

It was only then that Mr. Virtueson explained to Grandpa the circumstances of how Mr. Rodriguez had turned down the farmhand job the night before, but now he had changed his mind and accepted. According to the phone conversation, he explained that the ranch hand job out west was no longer available; so he was temporarily accepting Grandpa's offer in order to provide for his wife and son. But what really excited Ace was that they were going to move that very day. "He kept emphasizing that it was to be temporary. I think he still feels he is taking a handout," added Mr. Virtueson. "His pride is at stake, and I know just asking for this job was humbling."

There was no time to discuss this further for an unusual commotion was coming from down the hall, something not normal for a hospital unless there was an emergency. Then Ace recognized the voices. It was Booker, J. Michael, and Miriam from Harmony School, and Mr. and Mrs. Thriftmore. Mrs. Thriftmore hushed the boys as they came through the door, but the quiet did not last long when everyone saw how well Grandpa was doing. Miriam had a potted plant, and the boys had balloons and a sack of cards—all for Grandpa.

"We had an art project yesterday," explained J. Michael. "Mr. Trueword suggested that everyone make a card for you, and some of our parents sent cards also. The cards are not all get well cards; some are Christmas cards." He paused dramatically, then continued, "Only fourteen more days, you know."

"Yes, we know," smiled Grandpa. "Are you ready for Christmas? Do you think we will have a white one?"

"Very possibly," answered J. Michael in his most sophisticated, overdone professor voice. "It seems we are getting much more snow this winter than most winters, and I am hoping it snows on Christmas Eve. I love the snow!"

Everyone laughed; then Ace had a wonderful revelation. With brows raised, he threw an inquiring look at his father and rolled his eyes in the direction of J. Michael, Booker, and Miriam. Mr. Virtueson knew what his son had in mind and he thought, *Why not? The more the merrier*, but to be official, he did have to make the announcement. "Listen up, please, everyone," he said, raising his voice a little and signaling the children to give him their attention. "Booker, Miriam, J. Michael, how would you like to go out to the farm with us today? Ace has invited some other friends, and you would have to do some chores, but then you could play and sled in the snow."

"Oh, yes," they said in a hushed but excited chorus of voices, and jumping up and down as if they were on pogo sticks.

"That is, of course, as long as you have permission," he quickly added, looking at Mr. and Mrs. Thriftmore.

How could parents turn their children down for such a treat? Immediately Mr. and Mrs. Thriftmore gave their permission for Booker to go, and a couple of phone calls settled things for Miriam and J. Michael. Mr. Virtueson's cell phone had come in handy again.

"My friends from school will surely be surprised when they see who else is coming." Ace said, smiling broadly.

Mrs. Virtueson had another thought. "I just hope Grandma won't be too surprised when she sees all of us getting out of the van. She is likely to faint. She was expecting three for lunch, not twelve; but then again, she always fixes plenty."

That comment brought a smile to Grandpa's face. He knew his wife better than anyone. "Give her a call on your phone, son," he said, addressing Mr. Virtueson. "I have an idea she will think it is great, but a little warning would be considerate. Having to cook for a crowd will get her mind off me, and if a little more food is needed, she has plenty of home-grown canned goods in the basement. More hands will get the work done more quickly." So it was settled. Grandma would have twelve helpers instead of just three.

"The church van is a fifteen-passenger van," chuckled Mr. Virtueson. "Does anyone else want to go?" Then he remembered, "Oh, sorry. I didn't count Wags and the cleaning supplies. I guess once we pick up the others around town, we will be all filled up."

Everyone laughed heartily at that, even Grandpa. However, Dr. Harding, who was coming down the hall, heard the laughter and grumbled to himself about these people having too much fun, and if they had his troubles, they would not be laughing. He was on his way to the room to tell them to be quiet because they were in a hospital, but before he got there everyone was leaving.

What's the big joke and why the rush? he wondered depressingly. *I will be glad when that old man leaves. He has too much influence on people and things around here. He gets all this attention, and I could probably have a heart attack or drop dead and no one would even notice.* Although he would never admit it, it made him sad and more than a little envious toward Grandpa.

CHAPTER 12

HELPING HANDS

When the van arrived at the farm and everyone scrambled out, Grandma was beaming. "What a wonderful treat!" she said, putting her hands to her cheeks happily. "There will be plenty of food for everyone. We will eat at 12:00 sharp." She had everything under control. "I have chores planned. There are buckets, brooms, and the vacuum cleaner is ready, and there are plenty of rags and cleaning supplies. I want to put out clean towels and make certain everything is ready for the Rodriguez family. Girls, if we get the cleaning done early, you can help put up some Christmas decorations. I want the house to be full of Christmas cheer and a welcome sight when Grandpa comes home Monday. It will help him get well." Everyone agreed with Grandma.

It had turned out to be a beautiful day. Clean snow covered everything and clung to the tree limbs. Big icicles hung from the house and barn eaves, and they were growing even larger as the sun melted snow off the roofs. It was still a cold day, but the sunshine felt warm on faces. "Very invigorating," Grandpa would have said, had he been there.

"Come on, Dad. Let's go to the barn and see what needs to be done there," encouraged Ace. "It is obvious Grandma has everything under control here at the house." The boys were anxious to get the chores done so they could play. As they stomped through the snow to the barn, it crunched under their feet and flew off the heels of their boots. Wags ran ahead, and his tongue lolled out with clouds of steam puffing from his mouth and nostrils. No doubt about it, he enjoyed all the open space and freedom of the farm.

Out in the barn the chores went well. Mr. Virtueson cleaned the stalls while the boys carried armloads of clean straw for bedding. Of course, they had to stop and pet the sheep and the new calf after each load. When Hapford and Pudge put straw in the goats' pen, each goat struggled to get attention. They bleated and pushed against each other, trying to jockey into position where they could get the most strokes on their nubby heads. A mother cat with her kittens was also in the barn, and she kept a close eye on Wags, but he had better things to do than chase cats.

It took many armloads to give each animal a good bed. "This is hard work," said Pudge, "but it is fun too, and the animals seem to appreciate what we are doing."

"I don't think animals know how to appreciate," said Booker rather doubtfully. "They just like to be petted."

He stroked the calf's head, and she stuck out her long pink tongue and licked him. Then she tried to suck his finger. "Hey," he chortled. "Dinner will be here soon."

"It is cold outside, but it seems warm in here," noted Racer in a questioning tone. "I wonder why it stays so warm?"

"Tight doors, good insulation, and the radiant body heat of the animals," observed Reginald. He always had a logical, scientific reason for everything.

That made Hapford think. "Baby Jesus was born in a barn," he mused. "If it was like this one, it would not have been so bad, would it?" His simple questions could be quite thought provoking.

"Grandpa does everything he can to make the barn nice for his animals," said Ace, "but I do not think the stable in Bethlehem was nearly as comfortable and warm."

Reginald took the opportunity to share some of his expertise. "Bible scholars assert that the Christ child was really born in a cave, which would have been quite drafty," he explained. "Tourists to present-day Bethlehem can visit a cave supposedly similar to the one where He was born."

"Are there sheep and cows in it?" asked Hapford.

"No," answered Reginald emphatically, "and they have taken out all the hay and bedding as well, and to make it more appealing to tourists, they have strung electric lights, but I personally believe it has destroyed the aesthetic qualities of the site."

"How do you know all this?" asked J. Michael. "Have you been there?"

"No, but I have critiqued some photos in a travel book and researched it on the computer."

Hapford had another surprising, but simple, observation. "If there are no animals and no hay or bedding, it must not smell like a barn either."

"Say, it really wouldn't, would it?" reflected Pudge. "Maybe Grandpa's barn is more like where baby Jesus was born than that cave in Bethlehem. I think a barn is nice, and I like the smell of the animals and the hay and the straw."

"You may like the smell," said Racer. "Personally, I am not so fond of that part. As for sleeping here, help yourself. I'd rather sleep in my comfortable bed in my own bedroom."

Mr. Virtueson happened to overhear what the boys were discussing. "Sleeping in a barn is not necessarily distasteful. When I was small—about three or four—Dad would take me with him to the barn when he bedded and milked the cows at night. That was before there were electric lights in the barn, and we had to carry a lantern, which was the only light. I always stayed close to him, and sometimes, while he was milking the cows, I would lie down in the hay in front of them. I would fall asleep right there with the cows contentedly munching hay around me."

"Weren't you afraid?" asked J. Michael.

"No, cows as gentle and contented as Grandpa's do not bite."

About that time the boys heard Grandma ring the dinner bell. "That was good timing," noted Mr. Virtueson. "I believe you boys have done a good job of bedding the animals. Now, let's go in and wash up because I am sure Grandma has a nice lunch for us."

Mr. Virtueson was right. Grandma had started out cooking a pot roast, but that was before she knew Ace was bringing friends. When Mr. Virtueson called and told her to plan for twelve, she knew the pot roast would not be enough, but it was still not a problem. *We will have homemade vegetable soup,* she thought to herself. *I'll just add some tomato juice and a few jars of my canned vegetables, and I'll bake hot rolls and a big peach cobbler. I think that will be fine.* She was right!

As soon as lunch was over, everyone thanked Grandma for the delicious food. The boys were ready to go out and play in the snow, but Mr. Virtueson said they had to wait a while. It would not be good to be flopping down on sleds with full tummies.

Again Grandma was in command with a ready plan of action. "Dear," she said, addressing her son, "would you and the boys be so kind as to put up the Christmas lights around the front windows and along the porch banister? I want them burning brightly to welcome Grandpa when he comes home Monday."

Mr. Virtueson led the boys away. They were happy to help and decided stringing lights was more fun than sitting around waiting for lunch to digest.

Grandma had not forgotten about the girls either. "Do you think the three of you can handle the dishes and clean up?"

"Certainly," they answered together. "May we bake cookies after we finish?" asked Sandy. "We finished all the chores you gave us."

"I was going to suggest that," answered Grandma. "I already have sand tarts mixed up. They are in the refrigerator, and there is colored sugar and other decorations for them. Just be sure to slice them very thin."

"I will be glad to supervise," suggested Mrs. Virtueson, for she knew they might get carried away with sampling the yummy cookie dough.

"Thank you, Deary," said Grandma, using her pet name for Ace's mother. "In the meantime, I will just run upstairs and lay out towels and make certain everything is ready for the Rodriguez family, for I expect them any time. I am so grateful they have accepted our offer for employment."

When the Rodriguezes' blue sedan finally came up the lane, the house was a hive of activity. The boys had just plugged in the lights to see if they worked—which they did—and wonderful smells were coming from the kitchen where the third pan of cookies was being pulled out of the oven. Grandma was mixing up another batch of ginger cookies, but when she heard the car pull up, she dropped everything, wiped her hands, and went out to greet her new guests.

It did not take the Rodriguezes long to move in because they had only a few suitcases—all the belongings they owned. When Grandma showed them their rooms, big tears gathered in Mrs. Rodriguez's eyes.

"Oh, Grandma Virtueson! This is so nice, and everything is very homey. It is nicer than any place we have ever lived. We appreciate this more than you will ever know. Eduardo will do a wonderful job with the farm chores, and I will help you with whatever you need."

"Now, now," soothed Grandma. "Just get settled first; then we will talk about the rest."

As soon as Grandma saw that Mrs. Virtueson, Sandy, Christi, and Miriam had plenty to do decorating the sand tarts and baking up the ginger cookies, she decreed it was time to give Mrs. Rodriguez a grand tour of the house. In her welcoming, graceful manner, she put her new friend at ease and made her feel at home. She pointed out the linen closet, the laundry room, the closed-in back porch, and the little sitting room, which Grandma suggested they might use as their private family area while they were at the farm.

To assure Mrs. Rodriguez that feeding three extra mouths would not be a problem, Grandma also showed her the root cellar with its barrels of apples, onions, carrots, and potatoes. Then there were the pantry shelves crammed with canning jars of green beans, beets, corn, and other vegetables, as well as all kinds of pickles and relishes; and, of course, the fruits, like peaches, pears, and cherries, not to mention the jams and preserves.

"We have sides of beef and a lot of trout in the freezer and hams, bacon, and sausage out in the smokehouse. Anytime we want chicken or turkey, that is available for the catching and dressing," Grandma said with a good-natured chuckle.

"You have so much," declared Mrs. Rodriguez. "Surely you and Grandpa can't eat it all. What on earth do you do with it?"

Grandma's face beamed as she answered. "That is the wonderful part. The Lord allows us to share it with folks like yourself. Out here in the country, as well as in the surrounding communities, there are always those who need a helping hand at times. Grandpa and I don't have a lot of money, but we have always had good health and lots of energy to plant a large garden, can and freeze fruits and vegetables, and even make lots of jellies and jams. The orchards have done well, and the livestock has prospered under Grandpa's skilled hands; so, God has blessed with more than enough to supply our needs. He gives all this so that we can share. Your coming is at an especially blessed time—the Christmas season. You see, I am already preparing for the food baskets that Grandpa and I usually deliver two days before Christmas. Right now we are praying that God will show us the folks who should get one."

By then they had reached the kitchen again, and Mrs. Rodriguez was so overwhelmed she could hardly choke back the tears. All she could manage was a whispered, "God bless you, and thank you. Thank you for helping us get a fresh start."

Grandma put her arm around her new friend's shoulders and again soothed, "I am the one who is grateful, and I am very glad you took us up on the offer to help out."

Having finished up in the kitchen, the girls and Mrs. Virtueson went to the attic where they found and carried down the boxes of Christmas dishes and decorations stored there. Each was labeled with its contents and carefully packed. There were also big red bows, which would go on the spruce and hemlock Christmas wreaths for the windows. "Grandpa is very fond of the smell of fresh spruce and hemlock," explained Mrs. Virtueson. While the girls pressed and laid out the bows, she set out mulberry and evergreen-scented candles. Some went on top of the bookshelves and beside the fireplace, while others ended up as part of a lovely, holiday centerpiece on the sprawling dining room table, which was covered with a green tablecloth and red, green, and gold plaid napkins.

The girls eventually found the box marked "crèche" and started unwrapping Grandma's treasured olive-wood figures. Mrs. Virtueson said the set had belonged to Ace's great-grandmother and had been in the family for over one hundred years. "Things that help us feel connected to relatives are special treasures," explained Mrs. Virtueson. The girls lovingly handled and polished the Baby Jesus in his tiny manger, and there were little figures of sheep, cows, and even a donkey. The shepherds were there and so were some angel figures. Even the stable was made from beautifully carved pieces of rich-grained wood.

"But there aren't any wise men," remarked Sandy.

"No, because they did not come to the stable. Remember?" reminded Christi. "Let's put the crèche in the center of the fireplace mantel. Would that be an appropriate place, Mrs. Virtueson?"

"That is where Grandpa would want it. That way, everyone can see it, and it makes a good conversation piece, especially when visitors show up. Like Sandy, they often ask about the wise men, and that gives Grandpa an opportunity to tell them the wonderful truths of the Christmas story."

Grandma finally finished her tour with Mrs. Rodriguez, and the two of them came to see what the girls and Mrs. Virtueson had accomplished. They all stood back to admire the results. "Everything looks lovely," said Grandma, "and I am certain Grandpa will be encouraged when he comes home Monday. Christmas is his favorite time of year."

While Grandma was familiarizing Mrs. Rodriguez with the routines in the house, Eduardo visited the barn with Mr. Virtueson. "This is amazing," he said at one point. "In Puerto Rico the animals stay outside all year around. If they have a few shade trees or an open shed to sleep and feed under, it is the sign of a prosperous farm. Here, all the farms have barns, and they are huge barns with separate stalls or pens for all the animals. This barn even has two floors. The animals are downstairs in the stable, and upstairs there is equipment, lofts of hay, and bins of grain. I can see I will have more to do than just milk cows and gather eggs."

"Will that be a problem?" asked Mr. Virtueson.

"No, no," said Mr. Rodriguez. "In fact, it makes me feel better. I suspected that your father was just giving us another handout, but now I see he really does need help." By his tone, Mr. Virtueson sensed that Eduardo was warming to the help that Christians were trying to offer his family, although pride and self-sufficiency were still evident. "I will earn what I get, though, and I do not want charity," he added emphatically.

Here was a clear opportunity for Mr. Virtueson to tell Mr. Rodriguez about a gift that truly was free and could not be earned, but he approached it gently. "I appreciate your attitude, Eduardo. Not everyone is so sincere, or so willing to work hard. But surely you do not expect your wife and Manny to earn their Christmas gifts."

"Of course not. That is different. My gifts to them are my way of showing them I love them and want to provide for them." Then a coldness crept into his eyes. "I know where you are going with this," he said with a touch of snideness. "You are going to tell me God gave His Son to die on the Cross as His love gift to me. Well, I have heard all that before, Mr. Virtueson, so I do not need to hear it again. When I become a better person and am ready, I may make a commitment; but right now, God will have to wait. He has waited this long, hasn't He? You and your family have been very kind to give me this job, but please don't spoil our relationship."

There was nothing more Mr. Virtueson dare say. At least Mr. Rodriguez knew his need. Those who loved him, and knew the Lord, could only pray that he would not wait until it was too late.

CHAPTER 13

WAGS

All afternoon the boys stayed outside playing in the snow. Manny was as warm and snug as the others because his new friends at Harmony Chapel had dug into the missionary barrel and found some winter garments for him. They had discovered a striped stocking hat with a scarf and mittens to match. Best of all, there had been a one-piece snowmobile suit that fit him perfectly, along with a pair of boots. The sun was shining, and as the boys ran and tumbled in the snow and pulled their sleds up the hill, they hardly noticed the cold.

Wags was running around with them and enjoying himself immensely. Manny was overjoyed to finally get to meet the wonderful dog Ace had described in the hospital waiting room. "Look at Wags!" he exclaimed. "How I would love to have a dog like him! Here, boy. Come here. Let me pet you." He knelt in the snow, and Ace was surprised that Wags responded so enthusiastically. When his pet licked Manny on the chin and jumped to follow him, Ace felt a twinge of jealousy. That was all it was, though, just a twinge.

Ace did not mind sharing Wags' affection with Manny, and there was something else to consider. Since the family planned to move Wags out to the farm in the spring anyway, maybe he should be moved sooner now that Manny was here. That way Wags would have the freedom and space he needed, and Manny would have a pet to care for and play with. Wags would just be on loan though.

For sure, there was one thing Ace did not want to do, and that was to mention the idea to Manny just yet. He had to have his father's permission first, and he certainly did not want his new friend to get his hopes up falsely, as he had over the idea of Reginald searching for relatives on the computer. Manny should not be disappointed again.

Before they all knew it, the sun was racing toward the high, pine-forested mountain to the west. Mr. Virtueson called for the boys to brush off before they climbed into the van for the trip home, and he handed Ace a broom. The boys took turns sweeping snow from each other's clothes, and they shook out their hats and clapped their hands together to get the snow off their mittens. Mr. Virtueson did not want snow in the van, but even more, he did not want it melting on their clothes. Wet clothes could lead to colds and sore throats.

Back in the kitchen the girls were bundling up, and Mrs. Rodriguez and Grandma were putting sand tarts and ginger cookies into plastic bags. They would make a great snack for the trip home.

"Time to load up," Mr. Virtueson finally announced as the girls came out carrying two big bags of cookies. The boys helped the girls in first; then they climbed in after them. All the while, Wags had been sitting on his haunches at Manny's side, just watching. His tongue was hanging out and he panted contentedly. He almost looked as if he had a grin on his face, and every once in a while Manny would reach down and pet his head.

Finally, all the children and the leftover cleaning supplies were packed in. "Come on, Wags. You too," called Mr. Virtueson, snapping his fingers and making a sweeping gesture for Wags to jump up into the back of the van and into his carrying cage, but Wags trotted off toward the barn with his tail between his legs.

"Wags, come back here," commanded Ace from inside the van.

Mr. Virtueson started after the pet, and Wags turned and faced him; but instead of coming, he started zigging and zagging back and forth as if he wanted either to play or to avoid being caught. Each time Mr. Virtueson reached for his collar, Wags would sidestep the other way. Obviously, he did not want to get into the van or his carrying cage. Finally, in frustration, Mr. Virtueson said, "What is wrong with you, Wags? You act like you would rather stay here than go home."

"Ruff-f! Ruff-f!" barked Wags.

"Well, I'll be," said Mr. Virtueson. "What shall we do with you?"

"Come on, Wags," called Ace again.

"Could you let him stay?" asked Manny with a bit of a plea. "I will take good care of him."

Mr. Virtueson looked from Manny to Ace to Wags. He had a problem, but Ace knew he had a solution because he remembered what he had been thinking about earlier; however, was he really ready to let Wags stay at the farm? That was the dilemma. That little twinge of jealousy began to rise again, but Ace pushed it aside. Finally, he said, "It will be okay, Dad, because I really want what is best for Wags. I can't blame him for wanting to stay here on the farm where he has plenty of room to run and play, and we all knew it was going to happen sooner or later. I suppose Wags is just telling us now is the time. I will certainly miss him, but we will be out to visit at least once a week, so it is not as if I will never see him again. Staying on the farm is best for him."

It was settled. Wags would stay at the farm. Ace went home a little sad, but Wags was content; and Manny, well, he was thrilled.

CHAPTER 14

HOMECOMING

Monday was a wonderful, exciting day. After a hearty farm breakfast, Mr. Rodriguez drove his son to Harmony School and told him he would pick him up after school. Manny was not a visitor any longer, but a student just like all the others. He belonged and it was a wonderful feeling.

The distance from the farm to Harmony was not all that far, and it was an enjoyable trip on that crisp Monday morning with father and son chatting pleasantly. "The milking and feeding went well," said Mr. Rodriguez. Manny could not remember when he had seen his father more relaxed and satisfied. "There are some other chores to do when I get back, but I have the rest of the day to complete them." Then he chuckled, "You know, Wags was right there on my heels all the time—except when you were feeding him. I'm really surprised at how well he fits into the farm. Some city dogs would bark or nip at the cows and other animals, but Wags doesn't. Obviously, Ace has taken him to the farm quite often and has trained him how to behave around the farm animals."

"Ace is a good master, and I am trying to treat Wags just as well as he does," said Manny.

"It looks to me like you are doing a fine job. I am sorry we have never been able to have a pet for you. It is just that we have moved around so much."

"I understand, Daddy."

Mr. Rodriguez continued humbly, "I am thinking that if everything works out here, perhaps I can find a permanent job somewhere as a farmhand. I suppose we all know I am better suited to be a farmer than a cowboy." No more needed to be said as father and son looked at each other knowingly and smiled.

Just a little later that morning at the farm, Mr. and Mrs. Virtueson swung into the short, gravel lane. The car had not even come to a complete stop, when Grandma came bustling out the front door of the farmhouse. She was still tying a scarf on her head, but she was all ready to go. It was Monday morning, and if Dr. Kerrington was true to his word and Grandpa had progressed as expected, he would be discharged from Highland City Hospital that morning. The three of them were going to go pick him up.

Addressing Mrs. Rodriguez and waving good-bye at the same time, Grandma said, "Please be certain the Christmas lights are turned on, Marilyn. I want Grandpa to feel the holiday cheer when we drive up, and I also want him to see that the job is done so that he will not have to be concerned about it."

Mr. Virtueson backed out of the driveway and headed for town. It had turned out to be another sunny day, and the roads were clear and dry even though snow still covered the fields and lay in drifts along the snow fences.

"The weather certainly is quite different today from what it was the night the ambulance took him in," Grandma observed. "We never dreamed how much our lives would change with that trip, but I praise the Lord for His goodness. It is amazing how He can work through what we may think to be a tragic situation and allow it to become a blessing. Just think, if Grandpa had not fallen ill last Wednesday night, we would not have met the Rodriguez family. That had to be the Lord's providence."

"Yes, and you also might not have met that nice young man, Keith Hart," added Mrs. Virtueson. "Is he still visiting Grandpa every day? He seems to find in Grandpa some of the male leadership he has missed in his life. It is such a blessing to have a grandparent or some older family member to look to for direction and spiritual guidance. Our family is especially blessed in that way."

Mr. Virtueson picked up and continued the conversation. "When you say that, Dear, I immediately think of Manny. Ace said it really bothered Manny when his father refused to let Reginald use the computer to try to find out if he possibly has any aunts or uncles or cousins still living."

Mrs. Virtueson nodded, acknowledging that she knew about the situation and sympathized. Then she added, "I have noticed that Keith and Manny are hitting it off pretty well. It's good for both of them to spend time together."

When they reached the hospital, Grandpa was sitting in a chair in his room—all dressed, waiting, and tapping his foot in a rather restless, fidgety way. Dr. Kerrington was coming down the hall and reached Grandpa's door at almost the same time the Virtuesons did. He nodded to them and smiled at Grandpa saying, "Are you ready to go?"

"I have never been more ready," answered Grandpa brightly, with anticipation showing in his voice.

Dr. Kerrington put his stethoscope in place, bent over, and listened to Grandpa's heart one last time. "That ticker sounds fine," he said smiling. "As soon as Nurse Loyalton comes with the wheelchair, she will take you to the office, and we can complete your discharge. I know you are anxious to be on your way."

"Yes, I am," declared Grandpa.

"I cannot blame you," said the kind doctor with a small chuckle. "Now, if you behave yourself and allow your body to fully recuperate, I expect many more prosperous years ahead for you. We must all be grateful for the scientific enlightenment God has given doctors for treating conditions like yours."

Just at that time, Dr. Harding was passing in the hall. He could not help overhearing what Dr. Kerrington had said. "Enlightenment, my foot," he muttered to himself. "What I have accomplished, I have done myself with hard work and sweat. God has never done anything for me except cause grief." Then he saw Nurse Loyalton coming down the hall with the wheelchair. Again under his breath he said sanctimoniously, "Well, hallelujah! Grandpa Virtueson must finally be leaving."

Mrs. Loyalton breezed through the door and Grandpa, rising to greet her, announced, "I really do not need a wheelchair. Look at me. I am walking just fine."

"Maybe you think so," she countered, "but it is doctor's orders. You may not be as strong as you think, and besides . . ." Here she smiled slyly, "it is hospital procedure." That settled it.

A few minutes later, as Dr. Kerrington had promised, the discharge procedure was taken care of and Grandpa was on his way home.

"Is it not a perfectly lovely day?" he commented, gazing out the car window as the winding country road led them home. "I believe when you have had a brush with death, you become even more aware of God's handiwork in things around you. Look at that snow, for instance—white and pure like the cleansing of the soul, which only God can give. And the sunshine—does it not make one realize how graciously God smiles down on us in mercy and love?"

"Yes, Dear, it certainly does," agreed Grandma with a sigh. She patted him gently on the arm. "God's mercy endureth forever."

Something else was also on Grandpa's mind. "Speaking of mercy, did any of you meet Dr. Harding at the hospital? He was Eduardo's doctor. If anyone needs to experience the mercy of God, it is that man. If I even mentioned God's name when he was in the room, he would cut me off like the radio. I don't know why, but I was thinking of him and praying for him just now."

They arrived at the farm, and as they turned into the gravel lane, Grandpa exclaimed, "Well, well, look at that! Someone has done my job for me and put up the Christmas lights. Now all we have to do is get the hemlock and spruce so the wreaths can go in the windows. Is the crèche on the mantel?"

"Oh, yes," replied Mrs. Virtueson. "We remembered your conversation piece. The girls set it out when they visited on Saturday, and Eduardo is working on the wreaths."

Grandpa just smiled. It was so good to be home again. Wags came running from the barn and gave Grandpa his final greeting of the morning.

"My, my, it is Wags. Did Ace leave him here for Manny to play with?"

"You might say it was more Wags' idea," said Mr. Virtueson, and he went on to explain the events of the previous Saturday.

In the house of the righteous is much treasure .... Proverbs 15:6

CHAPTER 15

TIME TOGETHER

With Grandpa home and the Rodriguez family moved in, activity around the farm picked up tremendously. Grandpa could not do chores, but that did not stop him from seeing what needed to be done. After Manny had been taken to school each morning, Eduardo and Grandpa sat down to discuss what needed to be accomplished that day. Of course, there were the usual activities of cleaning stalls, putting down fresh bedding, exercising the animals, and watering them; but there were repair jobs also needing attention. The barn door needed some new hinges, the plow blades needed sharpening, the steps to the granary needed some new boards, and grain needed to be ground and mixed specially for each kind of animal.

"Am I working you too hard, Eduardo?" asked Grandpa after just a few days.

"No, sir," Eduardo beamed broadly. "I am enjoying the responsibilities more and more each day. There seems to be more to running a farm here than there was in Puerto Rico, but it suits me just fine."

"You know, every time you mention Puerto Rico, it is as if a dark cloud comes over your head."

"It is not Puerto Rico," said Eduardo. "Puerto Rico is a beautiful place to live. It just reminds me of my father and the pain he carried and passed on to me." With that he reached for his wallet and sadly pulled out a picture—a torn picture, the one Manny had described to Ace in the emergency waiting room.

"Because of him," he said in an unhappy tone, pointing to the uniformed man in the picture, "I grew up without my mother and my brother. My father died many years ago; so my son has no grandfather, and he also has no grandmother or uncle. I can bear it, but it just isn't fair to Manny."

Grandpa spoke softly and with sympathy because he wanted to encourage Eduardo. "How do you know your mother and brother are not still alive? Manny's new friend, Reginald Upright, has volunteered to try to find them. Just think how wonderful it would be for Manny and for you if they were alive somewhere and you could be reunited with them."

"I do not want to find them," he said with finality. "It will just bring back all the painful memories—the memories I want to forget."

"I cannot fully understand your hurt, Eduardo," said Grandpa patiently, "but there is One who truly does understand. His Father turned His back on Him too, you know. It was my Lord. He took the sin of the world on

Himself, and when He did, His Father turned away. That is why He said, 'My God, my God, why hast thou forsaken me?' He understands how you feel."

"Stop, please stop, Grandpa," Eduardo said pleadingly, waving his hands back and forth in front of his face. "I am not ready. I am not ready to find my mother and brother, and I am not ready to turn my life over to God. Life is confusing enough right now. I don't need to complicate it with the Bible and church and all that."

Grandpa said no more, but he thought about it all day and prayed that somehow Eduardo would soon be ready and place his trust in God. It was still on his mind, when, later that evening, Manny was supposed to be doing his homework. He watched the young scholar pick up a pencil, then stare blankly into space as if he were having a difficult time concentrating. "Is there anything I can do to help you?" asked Grandpa finally.

"Would you drill me on my new vocabulary words?" he asked with a slight whine. "They just do not want to stick in my mind. I think it is because I cannot get the Christmas music we are practicing at school out of my head. I just keep hearing it over and over." Quite animatedly Manny sang, "'Hear the bells ringing, they're singing, Jesus Christ is born today.'"

"Oh," said Grandpa, "that sounds nice. When is the Christmas program?"

"This Friday night."

"Who will be singing?"

"All the students from Harmony School, and some of them have special parts. Miriam will be singing a solo, and J. Michael will be reciting a poem. It is called . . . oh, I better not tell you."

"'Oh, I Better Not Tell You,'" said Grandpa mischievously. "That is a strange title for a Christmas poem."

"Grandpa, you know what I mean," said Manny with a grin. "You will be there Friday night to hear us, won't you?"

"Well-I," said Grandpa thoughtfully. "I am not sure. Quite honestly, I doubt Dr. Kerrington will think it is a good idea. I do want to hear you children sing though." Then he became very thoughtful for a few moments. Finally, he smiled and started shaking his head up and down. "Yes, I believe I can come and hear you sing. Only I cannot come Friday night."

"Well, that is the only time we are singing," explained Manny again.

"Maybe not," said Grandpa reflectively. "I will have to check with a few people, but I think you can plan on another engagement."

"Where? When?" asked Manny excitedly.

"I cannot say just yet. You know, just like you could not tell me the name of the poem." He chuckled and Manny smiled and thought, *Grandpa is something else, but I really like him.*

Then, with mock sternness in his voice, Grandpa said, "Smiles will not get you out of learning this vocabulary, young man. Have you studied the words and their definitions?"

"Yes, I think I know them now. Go ahead and ask me one," replied Manny enthusiastically.

"Okay, how about the meaning of 'punctual.'"

"That means, 'on time, prompt,'" responded Manny with a victorious look on his face.

"Correct," said Grandpa, "and if you are 'punctual' for breakfast tomorrow morning, I will have more information about your other engagement. As soon as we finish these vocabulary words, I will make a call and set it up."

"Oh, good! You know how to 'motivate' me, don't you, Grandpa? 'Motivate,' " he repeated, "'to cause to act.'"

Grandpa laughed at Manny's silliness but continued asking vocabulary words. His mind traveled back to similar conversations with his son, who was now known to all the children at Highland Church as Mr. Virtueson. He had also had similar times with Ace, his grandson, on occasion. Being a grandfather certainly had its rewards.

The next morning Manny was up before the sun. First, he had to shower and get dressed; then he had to get his homework and other school things into his backpack. Finally, he went down to eat breakfast with the rest of his family and Grandpa and Grandma. As he reached the kitchen, his father, who had been out at the barn long before dawn doing the milking, was just coming in. He had brought back some fresh milk to be refrigerated and used later.

"I would not be upset if someone—" and he looked lovingly at his wife, "would make me a nice coconut cream pie or a chocolate pie."

Mrs. Rodriguez smiled back. "I would need some eggs for the custard and the meringue," she chortled demurely.

"I know some hens who will be glad to cooperate," answered Mr. Rodriguez.

Manny thought this was all silly, but the new tenderness he saw between his mother and father made him feel warm inside like he did when he drank hot chocolate. It seemed that since they had come to the farm, everything had grown better. His father was less tense and irritable; his mother was relaxed and happy; and Grandpa and Grandma made it really feel like family—extended family. Manny even had a dog—one he could take care of and one that seemed to like him. There was just one sad thing. In spite of how happy his father seemed, Manny knew he still did not know the Lord in a personal way. He had opened his heart to Grandpa and Grandma, but he still stubbornly shut out the One Who loved him most.

As soon as the breakfast blessing was over, Manny asked excitedly, "What did you find out, Grandpa . . . about our other engagement, I mean."

"Well, first of all, I called Pastor Gentle at Harmony Chapel to see if the school choir had an opening Christmas Eve."

"Christmas Eve!" said Manny in astonishment. "We cannot go anywhere Christmas Eve. That is when we go to the service at the country church." Then he paused as the truth of what Grandpa was suggesting began to fully dawn on him. "Oh-h?" he said with a question in his voice. "Is the choir going to sing at the country church on Christmas Eve?"

"That is the plan," said Grandpa, "and Grandma and your mother and father and Ace and his mother and father will all be there."

"So Pastor Gentle said 'yes'?" asked Manny with hopefulness.

"Indeed, he did," replied Grandpa. "Now finish your breakfast and go out and feed Wags so you won't be late for school."

"Yes, sir," said Manny with a happy grin.

CHAPTER 16

THE SURPRISE

Thursday evening Ace and his mother and father went out to the farm to check on Grandpa. Wags came running as soon as he saw their car, and true to his name, he wagged his tail back and forth like a flag to greet the family. Ace bent over to pet him, and Wags licked his face. That made Ace very happy, for he needed to know Wags was still his loyal dog. "How are you, buddy? I have missed you," he said, rubbing Wags under the chin, "but I also understand how much you love the freedom of Grandpa's farm."

Manny had also come out to greet Ace, and he saw how much his friend loved his pet and how Wags responded to his master. "I am taking very good care of him," he assured Ace. Then he rushed breathlessly on with more information. "He is very good around all the farm animals, and Daddy says you have trained him well. He also says I can have a dog of my own soon. I want him to be just like Wags." That was Manny, running on and on with all the news.

As soon as Ace and Wags had finished their greetings, Manny invited Ace out to the barn where Mr. Rodriguez was doing the evening milking. Wags, of course, tagged along behind. The sun had already set, and it was getting colder; the weather report predicted more snow was on the way.

Inside the warm barn, Mr. Rodriguez was milking the goats. He lifted the bucket of frothy goat's milk and poured it into a large, heavy, metal can. Then he set his low, three-legged stool down beside another nanny. All the while the mother cat was watching attentively. "Are you looking for a drink?" Mr. Rodriguez asked. The cat meowed loudly. "Please bring me Kitty's bowl," he said to Manny, pointing to a good-sized dish in the corner. "I will pour some of Nanny's milk into it." He did so, and said, "There, Kitty. Now go call your kittens to come for supper." As if she knew what he was saying, she again meowed loudly and four gray striped kittens came running. The boys laughed loudly, amused at the furry barn family.

"Say, let's go pet the new calf," suggested Manny. To get to the calf's pen, they had to pass the horse stall where Babe, Grandpa's workhorse, was champing away at his oats. That reminded Ace of what Grandpa had promised at the hospital. Manny would surely be surprised. "Has Grandpa mentioned to you what we get to do two days before Christmas?" Ace asked.

"No. What?"

"Well, you know Grandma and your mother have been baking and gathering things together for the food baskets." Manny nodded assent. "Grandpa and Grandma always deliver them two days before Christmas. Do you know how they deliver them?"

"I suppose with their car. How else would they do it?"

"That is one part of the surprise." Ace reached over the stall and scratched Babe on the back. "Grandpa always hitches Babe to the old sleigh that is stored in the back of the barn, and Babe pulls the sleigh to the houses."

"There is a sleigh here in the barn?" Manny asked in a surprised tone.

"Yes. It is in an unused stall, and it is covered with a tarp. Maybe that's why you've never noticed it. Do you want to know the other part of the surprise?"

"What?" asked Manny eagerly.

"Since Grandpa cannot drive the sleigh this year, my dad is going to do it, and you and I are going to carry the baskets up to the doors. What do you think of that?"

"Terrific!" declared Manny. They talked about the fun of riding in the sleigh and of all the food and goodies Grandma and Mrs. Rodriguez were preparing. "Those families will be so surprised," said Manny. "I have never been able to do nice things like that for people before. Giving is the best part of Christmas. Don't you agree?"

"Absolutely," declared Ace. But the word was hardly out of his mouth when a very unexpected, puzzling idea—a surprise gift he could give—flashed through his mind. *Surely not, Lord,* he thought. He did not mention the idea to Manny, rather, he determined to give it lots of prayer, and he really didn't think he liked the idea.

Totally unaware of Ace's internal dilemma, Manny began talking about his new friends at Harmony School. Then he remembered that Ace did not know about the special Christmas Eve service. "Guess what," Manny said. "Our choir is going to sing at the country church on Christmas Eve as well as tomorrow night. It was Grandpa's idea, and he lined it all up. He called Pastor Gentle, and Pastor Gentle agreed and said Mr. Trueword could drive the church bus so everyone could come. Isn't that great?" He caught a quick breath and raced on. "Grandpa says we should cut some fresh spruce and holly and decorate the church. We can put out candles and tinsel. Everything will look and smell wonderful. Aren't you surprised?" He had to stop because he was completely out of breath now.

"Oh, yes," said Ace with a chuckle, "and I'm surprised you don't suffocate yourself sometimes." They laughed together because Manny knew how he sometimes got carried away in his excitement.

Ace had a question to ask his friend now. "Has your father changed his mind about giving permission for Reginald to use his computer to search for your relatives? He asked me about it again today, and he is still sure he can trace them."

"You must tell him to forget it," said Manny. "Daddy has not changed his mind, and I don't think he ever will. But, I do not feel nearly so lonely now. The night of the big snow changed a lot of things for me." He went on, smiling broadly. "Just think, I met you and Grandpa and Grandma and Wags. I have new friends at Harmony School . . ." His words trailed off because Mr. Rodriguez was calling the boys. He had finished the milking, and it was time to go back to the house.

As soon as they opened the door, the smell of buttery popcorn greeted them. "Take off your coats and come join us in the parlor," called Grandma. "We made a little snack."

As the boys entered the parlor, Grandpa asked out of curiosity, "What have you boys been up to?"

"Just visiting the animals," said Ace, "and Manny has been telling me about the Christmas Eve service you have planned. He says the choir from Harmony School is going to be there. Did you know that, Mom and Dad?"

"We just found out," replied Mr. Virtueson.

"I have another surprise as well," announced Grandpa. "Keith Hart called a little while ago." He paused for just a moment and sighed a little sigh. "He is such a nice young man—so caring and polite." That was not all Grandpa had to say though. "He reminded me that Ace extended an invitation to come out to the farm, and he wanted to know if Saturday would be suitable."

"That would be great!" exclaimed Manny. "I can introduce him to Wags and the new calf."

". . . and the kittens," added Ace.

"Oh, yes," agreed Manny.

"He was really coming to see me," said Grandpa in mock seriousness. Manny got a sad little frown on his face. Then Grandpa continued, "But, of course, he did ask about you." Grandpa paused again to see how Manny would respond to that revelation. Grandpa just loved suspense. "He did not know you folks had moved out here to the farm. I shared with him how things have worked out, and I also mentioned your special Christmas program tomorrow night. He said he would love to come, but he is on duty. Since he still wants to see you sing, I invited him to come to our service Christmas Eve."

"Is he coming?" asked Manny.

"Yes, he is."

As the Virtueson and the Rodriguez families chatted over their popcorn, Mr. Rodriguez was especially quiet and pensive. No one thought much about it. He worked very hard around the farm, and they all just assumed he was tired; but Mr. Rodriguez was observing what was going on around him, and he was thinking. *It is really not fair that Manny does not have an extended family as Ace does. Am I just being stubborn? Could we have family somewhere out there? What if, by some miracle, my mother and brother are alive? Is there any possibility they could be folks like the Virtuesons?* Then he realized why the Virtuesons were such a close, happy family. He thought some more. *Could it make that much difference in our family if I were a Believer?* He continued to bat the ideas around, and finally he reached a decision.

As the Virtuesons were leaving, it had already begun to snow. The car had a powdery film of white on it, and Mr. Virtueson had to clear the windows before they could drive off. When they did, Ace waved from the back window until the car was out of sight.

"I hope we do not get too much snow tonight," said Manny gloomily when they were back inside. "I want to go to school tomorrow, and I certainly do not want the Christmas program to be canceled."

“I am sure everything will work out and be just fine tomorrow,” said Mr. Rodriguez assuringly. “Now come. It is time for you to go to bed. We will have some things to talk about tomorrow.” He smiled and ruffled Manny’s curly hair.

“Why can’t we talk now?” asked Manny.

“Because I want to talk with Grandpa Virtueson first,” replied his father.

CHAPTER 17

ANOTHER SNOW

When Ace hopped out of bed Friday morning, he immediately ran to the window to peek out. Just as he had expected, they had had another big snow. He wondered how much had come down and if it had been as big a snowstorm as the one they had the night Grandpa was taken to the hospital. Ace could not help but go over in his mind again how he had felt that night. He loved his Grandpa, and he knew things did not always work out well in such situations. Grandpa could have died, but, as Manny had said, the events of that night had changed many lives. At the time, there had been some doubts, but now they could all see it was providential, and God had made "all things work together for good" for all involved. It had been a good lesson for Ace—one he never wanted to forget.

Having seen what was outside, he went ahead and got ready for breakfast. He knew school would not be called off. They had not called off school the day after the other snowstorm, so they would not call off school today. Then, as further assurance the world was still functioning, he heard a snowplow go down the street outside while he was combing his hair. He continued reminiscing and wondering if there had been any new emergencies during the night that affected anyone he knew. It seemed snowstorms gave more opportunity for accidents and crises, and he thought of that more often now since Grandpa's emergency. He would never forget that night in the hospital emergency room. Maybe the paths of lives had again crossed for God's glory during the night.

By the time Ace finished his breakfast and was getting his lunch and schoolwork packed up and was putting on his wraps, Mr. Virtueson came in from warming up the car.

"It is going to be a pretty day after all," he announced. "The sun is up, bright and strong. The snow might even melt off the streets by afternoon."

"I am sure Manny will be glad to see the sun," said Ace. "Snowy streets and roads could keep people from coming to the Christmas program tonight. He said they were expecting many visitors and had invited the mayor, the city council members, the fire chief, and the chief of police to come."

"It sounds like they invited everyone," commented Mrs. Virtueson jovially. "I certainly hope they all show up. Harmony Chapel is a very important part of the Harmony community."

When Ace arrived at school, he saw Pudge and Hapford outside tromping through the snowdrifts. It looked like fun, so as soon as he could deposit his lunch and schoolwork, he was outside playing with them. Before long, Mr. McMercy dropped off Sandy, Bill, and Becky. Becky wanted to stay outside and play with the boys, but Sandy insisted she go inside so she would not catch a cold. Bill, although a little older than the other boys, joined right in and suggested they build a large snowman. He started packing a big snowball to start rolling for the bottom. While Sandy was trying to persuade Becky to close the door, Christi and Mrs. Lovejoy parked and headed up the walk.

"Did you boys shovel the walk and steps?" Mrs. Lovejoy asked.

"No, ma'am. Mr. Friendson did," Pudge answered.

"Well, he did a nice job and we appreciate it," she responded. "We will all be sure and thank him, won't we?"

"Yes, ma'am," the boys chimed together.

Christi had a very pleased look on her face. "We brought some Christmas cookies for green dot treat," she said, "and I made a special big one for you, Pudge."

Pudge blushed and the other boys raised their eyebrows.

"It is just because I sit beside her in the Learning Center, and I pull her chair out for her," he insisted. "She appreciates my being a gentleman." He wanted to change the subject.

Bill came to his rescue. "Forget the teasing. Let's get this snowman built," he called. "I need help lifting this part up and putting it on the bottom part." He had rolled another large ball to help form the second part of the snowman's body; so the others ran to help.

Before long, other students, including Reginald Upright, arrived. He knew Ace had been out to the farm, and he was anxious to find out if Mr. Rodriguez had given permission yet for the computer search. He wanted Manny to find his relatives, but really, the very thought of challenging computer detective work intrigued him.

As Mr. Friendson blew the whistle for the boys to come in, the ritual was the same. Stomp and brush! Stomp and brush! Take off and hang up wet coats, mittens, and hats. Each boy's hair was always mussed and electrified, and the girls always giggled.

As the buzzer for school to start sounded, Racer came rushing through the door. The others had missed him but did not know why he was almost late. "Something happened at the hospital which made Mom late getting home," was all he had time to tell them.

In the Learning Center, just as always, the children recited the pledges and sang a chorus. Mr. Friendson also shared a Scripture verse, and then it was time for prayer requests.

Ace was the first to stick his hand up.

"Yes, Ace," said Mr. Friendson, acknowledging Ace's raised hand.

"First, I want to praise the Lord." He paused, then continued, "It was just a little over a week ago when my grandpa had angioplasty, but he is home now and doing very, very well. I praise the Lord for Grandpa's healing, but please keep praying for Mr. Rodriguez, that he will become a Believer."

"Yes, let's do thank the Lord for Grandpa's recovery," said Mr. Friendson smiling, "and we shall certainly continue to pray for Mr. Rodriguez. Are there other requests?"

Racer raised his hand.

"Yes, Racer," said Mr. Friendson.

"I was almost late this morning because Mom got home late from the hospital. They had an emergency last night. One of the doctors collapsed while on duty. They are not certain what happened, and Mom did not share any details. She was very concerned, however."

"Do you know the doctor's name?" asked Mr. Friendson.

"I believe Mom said it was Dr. . . . oh, . . . Dr. Harding! Yes, it was Dr. Harding."

Ace gasped in surprise, and Mr. Friendson turned. "Ace, was he Grandpa's doctor?"

"No," answered Ace aghast. "He was Mr. Rodriguez's doctor. He is a very bitter, angry man who does not know the Lord."

"Then we certainly do need to pray for him as well. Maybe this will be the thing that will open his heart to the Lord. Let us also pray for Mrs. Loyalton. Perhaps God will give her another opportunity to share the Gospel with Dr. Harding."

CHAPTER 18

GOD IN CONTROL

As soon as Manny opened his eyes Friday morning, he, too, hopped right out of bed and peered out his bedroom window. It was on the second floor, and when he pulled back the lacy curtain, he could see a long distance, and what he saw caused him to gape and gasp. It was beautiful but disheartening at the same time. All around the house and in the surrounding fields, the ground was a blanket of white. Only here and there a bare sapling or a few stray cornstalks stuck up above the frosty whiteness. Again he was reminded of what a contrast the climate was as compared to the climate in Puerto Rico.

Manny did not know how deep the snow was, but it looked deep to him. Maybe it was as deep as it had been the night they got stranded in Harmony. Now he had come to enjoy the snow. Since he had warm clothes, the cold was not really a problem, but the timing for this snowfall seemed all wrong. This was the kind of snow for a Saturday when one could go sledding, or it would have been nice for Christmas day, but not for the day of the big Christmas program.

Just then, his mother knocked at the door and said, "Manny, are you up? Your father will soon be in from the barn, and breakfast is almost ready. He has something wonderful to tell you; so hurry and come down."

Why hurry? he thought. *There will be no school today, and if by some miracle there is going to be school, how will I get there? We are snowed in.* Nevertheless, he obediently showered and got dressed. He still had to eat, and, of course, he had to feed Wags. Maybe, if he could not go to school, at least he and Wags could play in the barn. Then again, maybe the Christmas program could be rescheduled, but that wasn't likely. The whole situation was very disappointing. "Is there any way?" he said half out loud and half to himself.

Instantly, a verse of Scripture popped into his mind. "Commit thy way unto the Lord; trust also in him; and he shall bring it to pass."

Breakfast would have to wait a few moments. Even Wags would have to wait, because Manny had something more important to take care of. He dropped down beside the bed, his shoulders drooped in shame. "Lord," he prayed, "forgive me. I got upset about something that is not in my control. You control the weather, and You knew it would snow last night just as You knew it would the night we were stranded in Harmony. I commit this day to You. Please bring to pass what is best for me and my family. I trust You to work out everything to be just fine as Daddy said it would be last night."

At that very moment, if Manny could possibly have known what God had already done and what He was yet to do, he would have been wild with joy and anticipation. However, he did not know, but at least now he was not disappointed. He had peace that whatever the day held, it would be best for him.

When Manny arrived at the breakfast table, his mother and father were already seated. Both were beaming happily. In fact, he did not know if he had ever seen them so happy.

"Your father has a wonderful surprise for you," said his mother.

Manny noticed that neither Grandpa nor Grandma was at the table. "Shouldn't we wait until Grandpa and Grandma get here?"

"They already know about the surprise," said his mother, "and they have decided to have breakfast in their room. I just took it to them."

To Manny, this all seemed very strange.

"Listen to your father's exciting news," encouraged Mrs. Rodriguez. She seemed about to tell Manny herself.

I can guess, thought Manny. *There is no school today, and they think I will be happy about that.*

"Son," said his father very seriously, "do you remember what I said last night? That I was going to talk with Grandpa and that everything would be fine?"

Manny nodded. He remembered.

"The reason I wanted to talk to Grandpa is that I came to a conclusion, and I made a decision. I finally settled the fact that I need the Lord Jesus Christ in my life. That is why I wanted to talk to Grandpa. I wanted him to open God's Word and show me what to do."

Suddenly, Manny forgot all about the snowstorm. He forgot all about the Christmas program. He barely heard what else his father was saying, because his heart was singing. "Daddy," he said breathlessly, "did you really ask the Lord to be your Saviour?"

Mr. Rodriguez nodded and smiled broadly with love and joy evident on his face. "I did, son. I surely did." He paused, then continued, "I have been very stubborn and unhappy for so long. Because of the hurts I felt I had unjustly suffered, it was as if I built a high wall of bitterness and anger around my heart. That wall kept God out, and it made me a very lonely and bitter prisoner so that I could not really be a loving and understanding husband and father. Can you ever forgive me?"

"Oh, Daddy!" responded Manny, about to burst with joy. "Of course I forgive you, and I am so happy. I am so happy that you have accepted God's only way to Heaven!"

It was a wonderful moment. Mr. Rodriguez reached first for his wife's hand and then for Manny's hand. "Let's thank the Lord," he said, "for this lovely breakfast, for His love and mercy in providing His Son as a love gift to us, for our wonderful family, and for this day that He has made."

It was all nearly more than Manny could take in. It would not have mattered if his mother had fixed fried cardboard, hot rocks, and sand for breakfast because he was so happy. At last his father was part of God's family. Now, his **whole** family was part of God's family—at least all the family he knew about. There was that sad thought again.

When breakfast was over, Mr. Rodriguez said, "About the snow . . . Grandpa says I can put the snowplow on the tractor and clear the lane to the road. When I was coming in from the barn, the county snowplow went by; so if we clear the lane, I can take you to school. You will be late getting there, but your mother will call and let them know you are coming. I believe we can make it by 9 a.m." Then he pointed out the window. "Look, the sun is going to shine today, and it is going to warm up and be nice. The roads should be clear and dry by tonight so that everyone will be able to get to the Christmas program. You children are ready, aren't you?"

Manny smiled. "We are ready," he said enthusiastically. At that moment, even if it had been blowing and howling and snowing outside, there would have been sunshine in Manny's heart.

So, while Mrs. Rodriguez called the school and Manny straightened his room, brushed his teeth, combed his hair, and gathered up his schoolwork, Mr. Rodriguez plowed the snow out of the short lane. When he had finished, he came back inside to get something warm to drink and make sure his son was ready to go.

As Manny sat across from his father at the kitchen table, Mr. Rodriguez pensively sipped his hot drink and said, "The Lord knows I am a proud, stubborn man." He pulled out of his wallet the torn picture that Manny had seen only once before. "All my life I have wanted to know the other two people who should be in this picture, but bitterness kept me from trying to find them." He looked at Manny, who was totally surprised; then continued, "Do you think Reginald is still willing to use his computer to search for our relatives? If he is, I give my permission."

Manny was again shocked and breathless. If there had been any doubt, this was true evidence that his father's heart had been changed.

"Reginald is ready and anxious," answered Manny, nearly overcome with excitement. "When Ace was here last Saturday, he told me so. What a wonderful Christmas present it would be if we could find them!"

Two miracles had taken place, and all the way to school, Manny was rejoicing. He was so glad he had committed the day to the Lord, and he wondered if God had anything else He wanted to do to show that He truly was in control.

When Mr. Rodriguez pulled up in front of the school, it was break time, and the children were playing under the watchful eye of Mr. Trueword who was sprinkling salt on the sidewalk. The boys were building two snow forts, and the girls were playing tag in a huge pie shape they had stomped in the snow. They all waved in Manny's direction, evidently glad that he had made it to school after all.

As Manny was getting out of the car, Mr. Trueword began signaling for everyone to go inside. With the others, Manny stomped snow from his feet and hung up his wraps. He was putting his lunch in its place when J. Michael walked by. "Are you ready for tonight?" Manny asked his friend politely.

J. Michael grabbed his throat and opened his mouth to answer, but only a scratchy, whispered "no" came out.

Booker came up just then and explained sympathetically. "He can't talk; he has laryngitis, and unless his voice gets better, he won't be able to recite his poem tonight. We are all disappointed." Then, as if a light bulb had flashed on in Booker's head, he added quickly, "Say, do you know any Christmas poems?"

"No," responded Manny quickly and flatly. Actually, he did know one his mother had taught to him, but he certainly was not going to say so. He was excited about the Christmas program and wanted it to go off well, but if he said he knew a poem, they might ask him to recite it at the program that night. The very thought gave him butterflies in his stomach. Singing in the choir made him nervous enough, but reciting a poem . . . well . . . J. Michael might like to do it, but not him.

Booker's question had so startled Manny that for a moment he forgot about his good news. When he did remember, there was no time to share it. He would have to wait until lunch, and by then he hoped Booker would forget all about a Christmas poem.

He picked up his pencil to begin working in his math PACE, when a little voice inside, which was his conscience, began to bother him. *You lied. You did not tell the truth*, it chided. *You said you did not know any Christmas poems, but you do.*

Manny argued with the little voice. *But if I tell Mr. Trueword that I know a Christmas poem, he may want me to recite it tonight.*

That is right, but remember what you prayed this morning?

There it was again—the challenge to commit his way to the Lord.

I cannot stand up before people, he argued silently. *I cannot do that.*

Then another Scripture popped into his mind. "I can do all things through Christ which strengtheneth me."

The battle went on inside him until nearly lunchtime. *Okay*, he finally thought. *I will tell Mr. Trueword, but, Lord, please do not let him ask me to recite my poem.*

At lunch, however, there was something even more pressing. He had to tell everyone about his father's decision of faith. He also wanted to tell them that his father had given permission for Reginald to do some computer detective work to try to find his relatives, but his friends were not nearly as overjoyed as he thought they would be. He could hardly hide his disappointment.

As long as Manny could remember, his father had been a bitter, unhappy man. Now their home would be different. Manny was very happy, and his friends' lack of enthusiasm could not change what God had done.

It was not that his friends were not happy for him. It was just that the Christmas program seemed so important, and there were so many details that needed attention. Were the spotlights in place? Were all the candles and greenery in the windows? Would there be enough coat racks for all the visitors? Did they have enough cookies and punch lined up? Then, of course, there was the fact that J. Michael was not going to be able to recite his poem. The little voice again prompted Manny: *Tell Mr. Trueword about your poem.*

Manny could stand it no longer. He gathered his courage and approached Mr. Trueword. "Have you ever heard of the poem, 'The Christ of Christmas'?" he asked.

"No, I do not believe I have," answered Mr. Trueword, showing some interest. "Can you recite it for me?"

"Well, I wasn't asking to recite it. I just wanted to mention it. It reminds me of J. Michael's poem. You know—about bells and all." *Now, why did I say that?* thought Manny. He wished he could take the words back.

"But I would like to hear it," continued Mr. Trueword insistently. "Please recite it for me."

Manny started, and as Mr. Trueword encouraged him with nods and smiles, he said the whole thing. Then before he could say no, Mr. Trueword was asking him to recite it that night at the program. When Booker, Miriam, and even J. Michael heard, they all agreed he should do it. How could he turn them down? If it had not been for these friends at Harmony, none of the wonderful things that had happened in the last week and a half would have become reality. *What have I gotten myself into?* he thought. The Holy Spirit reminded him, *Commit your way to me, and I will help you. You can do all things because I will strengthen you.*

CHAPTER 19

A VISIT TO THE FARM

Saturday morning, the day after the Christmas program, Manny woke up late. His mother and father thought he deserved to sleep in after all the excitement of the night before. The program had been superb and a great success with every pew in the church full. Even the mayor and the chief of police had been there. Since all the children had generated so much excitement at home, nearly all the parents turned out; and, of course, Manny's mother and father had been there.

Manny had been a little nervous when he had gotten up to recite his poem, but the butterflies had stayed under control, and he had remembered every line. God had strengthened him. Naturally, Mr. Trueword had explained why Manny rather than J. Michael was reciting a poem. The strangest thing had happened after the program when everyone was having Christmas cookies and punch—J. Michael's voice had begun to come back.

As Manny lay in his bed thanking God for the previous day's blessings, namely that his father had trusted Christ as Saviour and that God had helped him with the stage-fright butterflies, "The Christ of Christmas" was also going round and round in his head. The words flowed along so easily now and did not take near the concentration they had taken the night before. The melodic lilt and beautiful message stirred again all the familiar images of Christmas, which he was getting very excited about now. He imagined his voice rising and falling with emotion and feeling; his hands in gestures expressing the representation of the poet's words. He mouthed the words over to himself once again.

THE CHRIST OF CHRISTMAS

The Christ of Christmas now behold,
    The Christ of Christmas morn;
The One by prophets long foretold
    In Bethlehem is born.
He is God's Son, Immanuel,
    Our Saviour and our King;
Let every heart the tidings tell
    And with the angels sing.

The shepherds rest beside the sheep
    Upon Judean hill;
An angel choir disturbs their sleep
    With songs that echo still.
To Bethlehem in early morn
    The shepherds wend their way;

Their hearts rejoice, the Babe is born,
And sleeps upon the hay.

The wise men cross the deserts wild,
Their treasures rare to bring;
Beneath the star they find the Child,
A Babe and yet a King!
To worship Him and minister
As to a king of old,
They offer frankincense and myrrh
And treasures made of gold.

Rejoice! for Christmas comes again
Around the whole wide earth,
To spread abroad God's love to men
As seen in Jesus' birth.
While Christmas bells in gladness ring,
Ring out o'er land and sea,
Make Him your Saviour and your King,
To reign eternally.

The Christ of Christmas let us adore,
His praises let us sing,
And love and serve Him evermore,
This wonderful Saviour and King.

As Manny got out of bed, the rhythm of the poem seemed to carry him around the room. Eventually, he glided to the window and swept back the curtain. The scene was truly picturesque, painted by the greatest Artist of all. The sun was shining and a glittery crust of white sparkled all over the yard and surrounding fields. The only contrast came from the bare, black trees of the orchard and the big, red barn. Overhead the sky was clear and azure blue, without a cloud in sight. It was going to be another beautiful, glorious day. He noticed his father had sprinkled ashes over the shoveled path to the barn, and a group of birds were having a delightful picnic at the bird feeder. Wags was padding around near the barn door sniffing in the snow, and that brought Manny back to reality—the reality of his duty and pledge to Ace. He had promised to feed and take good care of Wags; so, he had best get at it.

When he reached the big farm kitchen everything smelled of yeast and spices. Grandma and Mrs. Rodriguez were stewing a couple of fat hens for chicken and dumplings, and they were also making rolls and cinnamon buns. "Would you like some breakfast?" asked his mother.

"Thank you, but not yet. I have to go feed Wags first," he replied, putting on his snowmobile suit, boots, hat, and mittens. Then he hurried out to the barn.

"He is really getting very attached to that dog," observed Mrs. Rodriguez. "I do not know what he will do when we have to leave."

"Do not cross that bridge until you come to it," suggested Grandma, patting her friend gently on the arm.

While Manny was feeding Wags, he remembered that Keith Hart was coming that day to visit, and that filled him with more expectation and excitement. True, Keith had said he was coming to visit Grandpa, but Manny hoped he was coming to see him as well. Even though Keith was ten or twelve years older than he was, they seemed to have a lot in common. They both knew the Lord, even though Keith had not become a Believer until he was past twenty. They both enjoyed helping people, and he suspected they both liked dogs. Then there was the fact that they were both on the thin side and had dark brown hair and eyes, although his complexion was much darker than Keith's. As Manny remembered what Grandma and his mother were fixing for lunch, he thought, *I have a feeling Keith and I will both share an appetite for chicken and dumplings too.*

Manny was surprised and very happy when Keith arrived early. While the chicken and dumplings were finishing, he had time to show Keith around the barn and introduce him to Wags. "He is one fine dog," said Keith, scratching Wags behind the ears. Wags just gave a bark as if he understood; then cocked one ear and looked at Manny as if to say, "Isn't he smart?"

Of course, Manny also told Keith the wonderful news that his father had accepted the Lord. Then he shared with Keith the very special news that Reginald had been given permission to do a computer search to try to find his grandmother and uncle. Keith tried to cover his true feelings about this by acting enthusiastic.

When the chicken and dumplings were finally ready, they had both worked up a good appetite, and as Manny suspected, they both added it to their "favorite foods" list. Keith wanted to know all about the Christmas program, which pleased Manny immensely. He explained how he had ended up reciting a poem, and Keith interjected, "You will be reciting the poem again on Christmas Eve at the country church, won't you? I want to hear it, but not until then."

There was only one sad thing that dampened all their spirits that day. Keith shared it later while Grandma was serving her warm cinnamon buns fresh from the oven. "I don't suppose you have heard what happened at the hospital," he said.

They all indicated they had not. "You remember Dr. Harding, don't you, Grandpa and Eduardo?" asked Keith, nodding in their direction.

"Of course," answered Mr. Rodriguez as he took a large bite of a warm cinnamon bun. Some of the icing drizzled down the sides of his mouth, and he rolled his eyes in pleasure. "He was my doctor."

". . . and I am sorry to say he wanted nothing to do with the Lord," added Grandpa, reaching for his hot tea, "but I have felt a deep burden for him, and I pray for him often." He sighed. "When I tried to share how God loves him, he always became very angry, and he really became upset when I wanted to pray with Eduardo. For some reason, he seemed to think we should take sides, and he wanted Eduardo on his side. It was all very strange."

Keith hung his head. "Then I know you will be very sad to hear this."

"Hear what?" questioned Grandma. Keith seemed hesitant to tell them.

"Dr. Harding collapsed in one of the hallways Thursday night. No one found him for some time, and when they did, he was unconscious. It appears he had a reaction to a new medicine he prescribed for himself to fight depression. When he fell he also struck his head on a cart and caused a brain hemorrhage." Keith sighed deeply. "He never regained consciousness . . . and . . . well," he paused, hesitating to say the next words, "he died."

Grandpa set his cup down hard, almost spilling the tea. "Oh," said Grandma with a gasp.

For a moment they all had to let the news sink in. Then Mr. Rodriguez reached over and took his son's hand and his wife's hand. His dark eyes brimmed with shiny tears. "Thank you. Thank you both for not giving up on me. Except for your prayers and God's wonderful mercy, that could have been me. I could have gone into eternity never knowing God's love and His wonderful Son."

Sometime later before Keith left, he did ask to have some time alone with Grandpa. Manny did not mind but took the opportunity to call Ace and tell him the good news about his father's coming to know the Lord and give him an update on how the Christmas program had gone. Ace was very excited for his new friend and said he could hardly wait until Christmas Eve when he would get to hear the choir sing and hear Manny recite his poem. As for the computer search for Manny's relatives, Ace had given Reginald the go ahead, and they both agreed it could turn out to be a wonderful Christmas present. Ace also asked about Wags and said he missed his pet very much; then he explained that his family was going to visit the next afternoon, and the boys agreed they would play together with Wags. Since the weather prediction was for another sunny day, they planned to get in some more sledding.

Meanwhile, in the parlor, Keith and Grandpa talked. Actually, Grandpa did most of the talking and Keith gladly listened. Eventually, Keith looked at his watch and announced he had to be leaving since he was going to be on duty again that night. He thanked Grandpa and Grandma for their hospitality and left to take care of his responsibilities.

CHAPTER 20

FUN AND PREPARATION

On Sunday afternoon, Ace and his family visited the farm as planned, and the two boys played with Wags and went sledding. It was obvious to Manny that Ace missed Wags very much, and Wags was certainly glad to see his master. That made Manny a little sad and maybe even a little jealous, but he understood because he would miss Wags if he were to go back home to Highland City. The boys also discussed Reginald's computer search for Manny's relatives and, of course, the traditional delivery of the food baskets. It was exciting to think that Christmas was just five days away.

Monday and Tuesday, the last two days of school before Christmas break, whizzed by as work was finished up and the mothers hosted Christmas parties for the students. An observing eye could not have missed the Harmony School choir putting the last polishing touches on their songs, and several children from Highland School excitedly announcing how their families were going to attend the service at the country church on Christmas Eve.

During this time, Grandpa was beginning to feel like himself again, although Dr. Kerrington said he still had to take it easy and let Eduardo do the farm chores. That was not easy, and Grandpa also had a hard time occupying himself while Mrs. Rodriguez and Grandma totally immersed themselves in the final preparations for the food baskets. They insisted all he could do was watch, and everywhere he looked around the kitchen and dining room he was tempted by food and goodies waiting to be put into the brightly-decorated baskets. The final assembly area was the dining room table, and it looked like a Christmas gift shop, while the whole house smelled like a spice rack.

Finally, Wednesday morning came, just two days before Christmas. It was time to add either a chicken or a turkey to each basket. Each family would get one or the other depending on its size.

The baskets were loaded and brimming over by 10:30 a.m. when the Virtuesons showed up. By then Eduardo had finished all the morning chores and had taken Babe out of his stall so he could hitch him to the old sleigh. Ace, Manny, and Wags were right there to help, with Grandpa watching and supervising. He insisted they use the special harness that had sleigh bells attached, and under his watchful eye, the boys fastened four big holly wreaths to the sides of the sleigh. With its shiny red body trimmed in gold filigree and with the big green wreaths attached, the sleigh looked super—just like a Christmas card.

Most of the folks to whom the baskets would be delivered lived on back roads near the sawmill on the other side of the mountain. Since it had been sunny all week and most of the main roads were clear of snow, Grandpa told Mr. Virtueson to drive across the meadow and use the old logging road along the side of the mountain to deliver the baskets. The runners of the sleigh just didn't work on gravel or macadam, but they worked great on crusty snow, and there was still plenty in the meadow and on the mountain. Manny and Ace said they hoped no bears lived along the logging road, but Grandpa assured them all the bears were hibernating. As soon as lunch was over, the sleigh was loaded with six huge, overflowing baskets. Wags was right there, wagging his tail in anticipation. He was going along too. The boys, all bundled up in their snow clothes, hopped in with Mr. Virtueson just as Grandma came running out of the house with a big quilt. "Take this along," she said, "just to be sure you stay warm. You can wrap it around your legs."

"You do have your cell phone, don't you, son?" Grandpa asked Mr. Virtueson. He found it somewhat humorous that his son kept up with it so methodically.

"Right here." He tapped the pouch that held it to his belt. "We will call after we deliver all the baskets and are headed home."

By that time Wags was getting impatient, and circling the sleigh, he gave an impressive bark. With that, Mr. Virtueson gently tapped the reins across Babe's back and the boys yelled, "Giddyup, Babe!" The sleigh, with its load of love and happy crew, started with a jerk but was soon gliding smoothly across the meadow, heading for the spruce-covered mountain.

Grandpa and Grandma along with the Rodriguezes and Mrs. Virtueson waved until the sleigh was out of sight, then they headed back toward the house. On the way to the back door, Grandpa noted, "They are predicting snow flurries by morning, but as clear and beautiful as that sky looks now, I see no problem with weather. Besides, they should be back before supper."

Once in the kitchen, Mrs. Virtueson announced, "Grandma and Marilyn, you just relax until supper time. I brought a big roast and some pumpkin and mincemeat pies. Let me take care of supper. You must both be exhausted after all you have done to get those baskets ready. They really looked beautiful, and I know some needy families will have a more blessed Christmas because of your efforts. It is going to be a wonderful Christmas for all of us."

CHAPTER 21

SAFE DELIVERIES

The afternoon passed quietly at the farmhouse while Mr. Virtueson and the boys had a pleasant trip along the old logging road. Even though the ground was still snow-covered, there was evidence of animal activity. A few rabbits scurried at the unexpected sound of voices and sleigh runners, cardinals and wrens scratched around under holly bushes, and there were many different kinds of animal tracks crisscrossing the logging road and leading off in all directions. Before 2 p.m., Mr. Virtueson and the boys passed the sawmill and came to the first house where they would deposit a welcomed food basket. Along other back roads and lanes that afternoon, they made five more stops, and by 4 p.m. all the baskets had been given out to grateful families.

With the last basket safely delivered, Mr. Virtueson turned Babe toward home, and the boys, full of chatter over the task they had just completed, settled in for the trip home. Wags was worn out, and without the temptation of the food in the baskets, he was allowed to ride in the sleigh as well. In no time, weary Babe reached the old logging road again and headed up the tall, dark mountain. As they went, the air began to grow raw, and snow began to fall rather heavily. It got heavier and deeper as they passed the sawmill again and continued further up the mountain. At one point Manny asked, "Are we in for another blizzard?"

"It looks like we might be," declared Mr. Virtueson. "The weather report only called for flurries, and not until late tonight. I believe I will give Dad a call, though, and let him know we may be later than expected because of this." However, the call didn't go through.

Things had been quiet and relaxing all afternoon at the farmhouse. Just past 4:30 p.m., Eduardo headed for the barn to do the evening chores, and Grandma looked out the kitchen window. Thick snow flakes were unexpectedly and ominously swirling across the yard between the house and the barn. "Oh, my," she said. "The weather report called for snow flurries by morning, but by the looks of things we might well be in for another real snowstorm, and it is here early." Her comment was somewhat unsettling to Mrs. Rodriguez and Mrs. Virtueson because their thoughts immediately turned to Mr. Virtueson and the boys.

A few minutes later Grandpa came into the kitchen. "Isn't it about supper time?" he asked. "The smell of that roast you have been cooking all afternoon is about to get the better of my taste buds." Grandma did not reply but just motioned toward the kitchen window. Grandpa saw the snow, and a great uneasiness began to rise in the pit of his stomach. "I think I'll see if I can reach our son on his cell phone. Maybe that gadget will come in handy yet."

On the other end he heard a ring and then a melodious voice said, "I'm sorry. The party you are trying to reach is presently out of the coverage area."

When Grandpa conveyed the message, Grandma responded with little comfort in her voice. "Well, all we can do then is wait. Maybe he will be able to reach us." The two mothers somberly nodded.

By 6:30 p.m., Eduardo had long since finished the barn chores, the roast and pies were untouched, and there was still no phone call or sign of Mr. Virtueson and the boys. It was snowing harder than ever, and the wind had picked up so that the snow was drifting. Grandpa had confidence that his son knew how to drive the sleigh through fallen snow, but he also realized drifts could present some unplanned challenges. Concern was mounting. He had tried several times unsuccessfully to reach his son over the cell phone, and Mrs. Virtueson could not understand why her husband had not called them. Finally, Grandpa felt they should wait no longer. He called Good Samaritan Rescue. He also called Pastor Alltruth in Highland City and Pastor Gentle in Harmony. Things had taken a turn for the worse, and they all agreed to spread the word for friends to pray.

The clock ticked on and everyone waited. When the team from Good Samaritan Rescue arrived, Grandpa quickly explained the situation—Mr. Virtueson had taken the boys with the horse and sleigh and gone over the mountain to distribute food baskets to several needy families. They had taken the old logging road because of the sleigh, but Grandpa did not know where they were now or why they were not back, and he had not been able to reach his son by cell phone. The rescue team decided they would take the main road and be able to reach the sawmill more quickly than over the logging road. After they reached the sawmill, they would try to determine whether or not the sleigh had passed.

They could not have been gone more than fifteen minutes when there was stomping on the back porch. Mrs. Virtueson immediately rushed to the door, thinking it must surely be her husband and the boys, but when she opened the door, everyone was surprised to see it was Keith Hart.

Grandpa quickly overcame his astonishment and urged, "Come in! Come in!" He pushed the door closed against the cold wind. "Whatever are you doing here in this weather?"

Keith stopped stomping but continued brushing off the snow. "This is definitely another blizzard," he commented. "As my partner and I were finishing our shift, we heard over our ambulance radio that Good Samaritan Rescue had been called out. When I recognized the address, I decided to come see if I could help in any way. Have they come back yet?"

"No," sighed Grandpa. "We can only wait and pray." While Keith and Grandpa retired to the parlor, the others decided the best use for the roast was to make sandwiches for the rescue party. They themselves certainly had no appetites as long as their loved ones were still out in the snowstorm.

As the minutes slipped by, Grandpa watched the clock, but Keith sat deep in thought. He was thinking mostly of Manny. Finally, he said, "You know, last Saturday when I came to visit you, Manny told me that his friend Reginald was going to use his computer to search for Manny's relatives. I know Manny is all excited about the possibility of finding some more family, but he might be setting himself up for a big disappointment, and I would not want to see him get hurt."

"What do you mean?" asked Grandpa.

"Well, a few years back I tried a similar search using an agency that guaranteed a 90 percent success rate for finding 'lost' relatives; but they said I couldn't provide enough information, so the search foundered. Getting my hopes up and then being let down was worse than not knowing anything. I just pray the same thing doesn't happen to Manny."

Grandpa looked confused. "Who were you searching for?"

"My father and my brother. There is a lot about my childhood that I've never shared with you, Grandpa. You see, I was only a baby when my mother and I left Puerto Rico, and it wasn't until I was older that she told me anything about my father or my brother. Also, Mother had our last name changed when we moved here, and she never told me my original family name. I guess she didn't want me to find my father."

"Did you say you lived in Puerto Rico?" Grandpa was astounded. "I thought most Puerto Ricans have darker skin, like the Rodriguezes. You are so fair."

"Not everyone from Puerto Rico has dark skin or speaks Spanish. Didn't I tell you that night in the ambulance that Mother and I came here from Puerto Rico to live with relatives?"

"I remember you talking about living with your aunt, but I must have missed the part about Puerto Rico."

"Mother was not born in Puerto Rico, and I took after her. That is why I am so fair-skinned," explained Keith. "Here, let me show you a picture of my mother."

Keith drew his wallet from his hip pocket and started flipping through some business cards and pictures. He stopped and pulled out one folded, faded picture and explained, "Mother gave me this picture before she died. That is me on her lap. I used to look at this photograph and try to imagine my older brother standing beside us." Grandpa leaned forward, straining to see the picture. A glimmer of familiarity struck him. Surely it could not be. "May I look more closely, please?" he asked in a very interested but cautious manner. "You know my eyes are not as good as they used to be." Keith handed over the picture, and Grandpa completely unfolded it, revealing a tattered, torn edge on the left. He gazed at the picture intently, taking in all the details of the background. What he recognized was astonishing, but to Keith, he simply said, "Part of this picture is missing."

"Yes, I know. This is the way it was when Mother gave it to me. I suppose she didn't want me to see what was in the rest of the picture."

"Thank you for letting me see it," said Grandpa simply. I believe I know much more about you now." All the while a warm feeling of excitement was rising within his chest. The very existence of the picture was truly amazing. During the last three weeks, God had been preparing a Christmas gift which it appeared He was going to allow Grandpa to deliver. Silently Grandpa prayed, *I believe you will bring my son and grandson and Manny back to us safely.*

At that very moment the phone rang, and Grandpa jumped to answer it. It was the command station for Good Samaritan Rescue. The team had found the sleigh part way down an embankment about two miles up the mountain from the sawmill. They had also found a quilt and a cell phone, but the horse, the dog, and Mr. Virtueson and the boys had not yet been located. The team would continue searching. Meanwhile, the roast beef sandwiches sat untouched and the hot drinks grew cold. Outside the storm had not let up at all; in fact, it seemed to be worsening.

As the mantel clock in the living room ominously struck 9 p.m., they all waited quietly, listening to the wind bluster outside. Mrs. Rodriguez clutched her husband's hand. A deep furrow had settled between her brows, and her lips were tightly pursed. At least a foot of snow had fallen outside, and the temperature had plummeted in the last two hours.

But the salvation of the righteous is of the Lord:
he is their strength in the time of trouble. Psalm 37:39

At first she thought it was just the wind, but then Mrs. Virtueson jumped up and shouted, "Listen, I think I hear Wags barking!" They all stopped and listened.

"It is Wags!" declared Grandpa confidently, hurrying to the door. Three very cold, snow-covered figures and a tired dog pulled themselves up the porch steps and nearly fell in through the open kitchen door. Behind them was the Good Samaritan Rescue team.

CHAPTER 22

A REASON TO CELEBRATE

There was much more to celebrate now than just the holiday. Ace, Manny, Mr. Virtueson, and Wags, along with poor, weary Babe were safe. The Good Samaritan Rescue team had not found them but had caught up with them as they were struggling home across the meadow.

The boys explained it all. "It was Wags and Babe who saved us," declared Manny.

"Really," said Grandpa in amazement, "and how is that?"

Mr. Virtueson explained how, after they had made all their deliveries, they had started back up the mountain headed for home.

"Then the blizzard caught us," interjected Ace. "It must have been as bad as the night you went to the hospital, Grandpa."

". . . and when our car broke down," added Manny.

Mr. Virtueson continued, "The sleigh would have done fine, if we could have reached the meadow," said Mr. Virtueson, "but the snow started drifting, and I could not always see the road. We slid off and I knew there was no use trying to get it back on the road. We just had to unhitch Babe and leave the sleigh. In that blowing, swirling snow we became disoriented and were not certain which way to go. When I headed Babe in one direction, he did not want to go, and Wags started barking. We finally decided to let them lead us home because the snow did not seem to confuse them."

"Well, I say . . . and you lost your cell phone, didn't you," added Grandpa with a sly, knowing grin.

"Yes, I did," admitted Mr. Virtueson, "but earlier I had tried to call. Evidently I was out of my coverage area."

"Praise the Lord! He does not have coverage areas!" declared Grandma. "His ear is always tuned to the needs of His children. We have so much for which to be thankful. Everyone is home safe and sound and the food baskets were delivered before the bad weather hit." She paused and wiped a tear from her eye with the hem of her apron and looked at Grandpa. "Dear, will you please just voice a prayer of thanksgiving to the Lord from all of us."

So the wind howled and screamed outside, but in the farm kitchen all was well as Grandpa's deep, reverent voice thanked the Lord for bringing Ace, Manny, Mr. Virtueson, the rescue team, and even Wags and Babe back safely. When the "amens" were all said, Grandma heated up the cocoa and coffee, Mrs. Rodriguez uncovered the sandwiches, and Mrs. Virtueson cut the pumpkin and mincemeat pies. Although the rescue team soon left in case they had other business that night, it was decided that Keith should stay over. The attic bedroom was ready.

The next morning at breakfast—as if no one would have remembered—Grandpa announced, "It's the day before Christmas." Ace thought Grandpa seemed unusually anxious for Christmas to arrive.

"And the day of the special service at the country church," reminded Manny excitedly. He seemed to have recovered from the harrowing experience of the night before amazingly well. "Do you think many will come?" He grabbed a quick breath and hurried on. "The storm seems to have worn itself out over night, and Daddy can plow our lane again and the parking lot at the church. We can go cut spruce and holly boughs, and Keith can help us decorate. Right, Keith?" He cast an assuming glance in Keith's direction and gave him a big grin before rushing on again. "This is going to be a wonderful Christmas Eve, isn't it, Grandpa?" They all laughed. That was Manny all right—just going on and on without hardly taking time to breathe.

Grandpa had that sly, knowing grin on his face again, and with prophetic words, he said, "It most certainly will be—one none of us shall ever forget."

With all the preparations, the day went very quickly. Mr. Rodriguez plowed out the lane and drove the short distance to the country church where he plowed the parking lot. After lunch, the boys and men—except Grandpa—went to the church and decorated with spruce and holly boughs taken from the many trees and bushes that surrounded the church. They also set out tall, angel-white Christmas candles and hung garlands of glittering tinsel. Everything was set and perfect to welcome the choir from Harmony School and the visitors from the community.

Back at the farmhouse in Grandma's kitchen, preparations were shaping up as well. The three women were sharing the tasks of stuffing the turkey, making more pumpkin and mincemeat pies, stirring up rolls and cinnamon buns, and washing potatoes, carrots, and other vegetables from the root cellar. As it had all week, the house smelled wonderful.

The day went by quickly, and nearly before Ace and Manny knew it, they found themselves at the church greeting Ace's friends from Highland City and, of course, the children and Mr. Trueword and Pastor and Mrs. Gentle from Harmony. On the windowsills, the candles, which were nestled among the holly, flickered elegantly; and the garlands, gracefully draped on the ends of the pews, shimmered and sparkled magnificently. The little church was full to capacity and brimming with joy for the occasion.

Finally, as Manny stood up, everyone grew quiet, and just as planned, he opened the program by reciting "The Christ of Christmas." After he finished, the choir sang a number, Miriam sang her solo, the choir sang several more selections, and then it was J. Michael's turn. Would the unpredictable laryngitis strike again? No; clearly and movingly, he recited every line without hesitation. The finale was followed by enthusiastic applause, and the audience requested the choir to sing it again, which they gladly did.

Afterward, Ace and Manny were congratulating and thanking their friends when Reginald came rushing up. He wanted to "express his immense gratitude for a superb performance," he said. Manny thanked him and asked with obvious anticipation, "Do you have any news about my relatives?"

Reginald hung his head sadly and groaned. He really did not want to tell Manny the bad news. "I had great expectations, my dear Manny, but it appears I have reached an impassable obstacle."

"An impassable obstacle?" questioned Manny. Then he turned to Ace. "What does he mean?"

"I believe he has come to a dead end," explained Ace.

"Precisely," said Reginald. "It seems that when your grandmother and uncle arrived in this land, they . . . well, they vanished."

"Vanished?" questioned Manny again. "How could they just vanish? Even if they died, there would be records of that."

"The most likely probability is that they changed their identities," explained Reginald. "If that is the case, I can go no further without knowledge of their new family name."

"Oh, no," said Manny with a deep sigh. His shoulders sagged, showing his disappointment. "I should have known it was too good to be true." Then he added gloomily, "I guess God just doesn't want me to have other relatives, but it sure would have made a great Christmas present."

"I am most truly regretful," said Reginald sadly. He had really thought the search would prove successful, and he didn't like seeing his new friend so downhearted. For Manny, it was a very sour note in an otherwise remarkable evening.

As the Virtuesons, Rodriguezes, and Keith trekked back to the farmhouse, Manny realized it was still a wonderful, blessed Christmas, and he had much for which to be thankful. God had certainly done great things for his family, and Grandpa reminded him again that God had brought them all together for a reason and predicted it would be a Christmas they would never forget.

Eventually, everyone gathered in the parlor, and as was the Virtueson tradition, the Christmas candles were lit, the smell of spruce and spices mingled in the air, and a warm fire crackled in the fireplace. Then Mr. Virtueson led everyone in singing Christmas carols, and Grandpa read the Christmas story out of Luke 2 and Matthew 1. It all gave Ace a warm feeling of love and security, and he was glad they could share this Christmas with Keith and the Rodriguezes. As he glanced at each of them, they seemed completely taken up in the solemnity of the moment.

Finally, it was time for hot, spiced cider and Christmas cookies. They were having quite an enjoyable time when Grandpa surprised everyone by saying he was going to do something he had never done before. "I have a family gift I want to share tonight," he said.

This was not the usual family tradition, and all kinds of thoughts went through Ace's head, but Manny thought it was very exciting. Grandma looked at her son and daughter-in-law as if to say, "Did you know about this?" and she encouraged Grandpa to continue. "What do you have, Dear? We are all anxious to see it."

"First," said Grandpa, "I would like to ask Keith to pull out the picture he showed me last night." Keith was puzzled, but reached for his back pocket as Grandpa continued. "Eduardo, please take out the picture you showed me some time ago—the wrinkled, faded one of you and your father."

Now everyone was even more bewildered. What possible importance could two old pictures have in Grandpa's giving a special family Christmas present? Nevertheless, both Keith and Eduardo went along with the seemingly meaningless exercise. Grandpa had been kind to both of them. They would humor him.

"Unfold your picture, Keith, and lay it flat on the table," said Grandpa. "Eduardo, please lay your picture beside it."

While Keith and Eduardo obeyed Grandpa's request, the others looked on with good humor. Little did they realize it would be a moment never to forget. Both Keith and Eduardo seemed frozen, staring at the two pictures. What did they see?

Then Grandma and Mrs. Rodriguez and the others saw. It was unbelievable! In truth, there were not two pictures lying on the table, but one picture—one picture torn in half years before, the two halves still fitting perfectly together.

In a way only God could work, He had brought together some very unusual circumstances to reunite two brothers after over twenty years of separation. As a gracious Heavenly Father, He had lovingly worked in each of their lives to bring them into the family of God and back to each other.

At first, Ace and Manny did not fully understand how the torn picture linked Keith and Eduardo, but Grandpa knew, and after the initial shock subsided, Keith and Eduardo put it all together. They were brothers! They held each other at arms' length; then they gave each other a big hug. They did not physically favor each other greatly because Keith had taken after his fair-skinned mother, while Eduardo had taken after his Puerto Rican father and had for twenty years been tanned by the hot Puerto Rican sun. The similarities showed up more in what Eduardo had passed on to his son Manny.

There were still so many questions, but the details of each other's lives over the years could be filled in later. For now, the picture was proof enough. They were brothers. Then Grandpa, with the widest grin Ace had ever seen, said, "Manny, meet your Uncle Keith. I know you wanted a grandfather, but an uncle is the best I can do."

What a joyous sight it was as uncle and nephew, who had already been drawn together for reasons they did not understand before, embraced. *No wonder Manny and Keith get along so well,* thought Ace. *It makes perfect sense.*

As the celebration and rejoicing continued, Ace thought about all God had done. He had not understood just two and a half weeks before, when he made the cold nighttime ride to the hospital, that God was going to use, what at first appeared to be, a tragedy to give him a new friend and to work out unbelievable circumstances to reunite a family. God truly was a loving Heavenly Father.

There was only one more thing needed to complete the celebration, and Ace, with thoughtful determination, knew what that was. He had been struggling with the idea since he had been at the farm the Saturday before, but he was sure what God wanted him to do now. It was not going to be easy, but it was the right thing, and this was the time to do it. "Now I have a special gift for Manny," he finally said, getting everyone's attention. "I was not certain I could give it, but I will, and I want to give it to him tonight like Grandpa gave his gift."

Everyone looked at the pile of presents in the corner and expected Ace to reach for one and hand it to Manny, but he did not.

"Where is it, son?" asked Mr. Virtueson. "Did you hide it?"

"It is in the barn," replied Ace. Then he turned and looked directly at Manny. "You have become a very special friend, and I could only give this gift to a very special friend." He paused and swallowed hard. "I want you to have Wags." Having said that short, difficult sentence, he swallowed again, cleared his throat, and went on. "Wags loves the farm, and he has come to love you. Wags will always be special to me, and deep down, he will always be my dog, but I know you will take good care of him. Grandpa says your father wants to continue doing farmwork either here or somewhere else. Either way, Wags will be on a farm and be happy. Hopefully I will be able to visit you both often. When I do, he'll remember me, and I will see that he is happy and that giving him to you was the right thing to do."

"Are you sure you want to do this?" asked Manny in disbelief. He was obviously overjoyed, but at the same time concerned about his new friend's feelings. He wondered if he could have given such a meaningful, sacrificial gift.

"Yes, I am sure," replied Ace. There was sadness in his voice, but also relief and anticipation. It was hard to give up his pet, but it was good to know he had done what God wanted him to do. "I believe one reason God allowed us to meet was so that He could give Wags a new home."

"It will be a good one," said Mrs. Rodriguez. She knew how much her son had always wanted a dog and how he doted on Wags.

Around the room, the candles still glowed warmly, but the fire had died to little more than embers. What a wonderful Christmas Eve it had been, and as Grandpa had predicted, one no one in the room would ever forget. However, it was getting late; so, just as he had done on all the Christmas Eves Ace could remember, Grandpa ceremoniously announced, "Well, I think it is time for you boys to go to bed."

As Ace and Manny headed up the stairs, they both had wonderful, warm, secure feelings inside. An unbelievable Christmas Eve had come and would soon be gone, but neither young man would forget that night. For Ace, it had been a lesson in the meaning of sacrifice. For Manny, it had been another testimony of God's loving care and mercy for His children.

Before either of them slid under one of Grandma's warm, cozy comforters, they pulled back the lacy bedroom curtains and looked outside. It was beginning to snow just as the weather report had predicted, and it was going to be another big snow.